safe with me

CINDY HOUGHTON

INDEPENDENTLY PUBLISHED

Copyright © 2024 by Cindy Houghton

All rights reserved.

No part of this book may be reproduced in any form or by any electronic or mechanical means, including information storage and retrieval systems, without written permission from the author, except for the use of brief quotations in a book review.

While the location is real, this story and its characters are fictional. They are not meant to depict in anyone or their history.

ISBN: 9798326099099

Edited by Chessa Andersen of Hawthorn & Aster

Interior Formatting by Ivy of Hawthorn & Aster (www.hawthornandaster.com)

content warning

Brief homophobic language (Prologue)
Substance abuse & addiction
Gambling

To all the outcasts, show the world what you've got.

prologue
TEN YEARS AGO

"That test was brutal." I press my head against the cool metal of my locker.

"You always say that." Sydney bumps my hip with hers.

I've been in love with her since we were partnered together in our freshman biology class. With Sydney Parker as my lab partner, suddenly getting to school on time was not an issue. I lived for the mornings of seeing her big blue eyes behind safety goggles and catching the subtle strawberry scent from her blonde hair.

It has been four years of loving all the moments we have together. Not that there are many since we run in different circles. She's a cheerleader and hangs out with the jocks. I'm the loner who disappears into the auto shop after school. I don't go to parties on the weekends, not that any of the snobs in this school would invite me.

But Sydney is different. She's popular, but kind and sweet. When others laughed about us being paired up, she just moved her chair closer to mine. We sometimes study together at the library down the street. She doesn't shy away from being seen around me.

Today, I'm going to tell her how I feel and ask her to the senior prom. I've been planning it for months.

"Noah? Earth to Noah." Her voice snaps me back to reality. "Are you ok?"

"Yeah, just thinking." I toss my books into the locker. "I need to get to the gym. Can you meet me after the last bell? I need to talk to you about something."

"Sure, but I can't stay long. I have cheer practice."

"Yeah, it will be quick."

She nods before walking to her last class. I probably watch for longer than I should. It's safe to say that watching her hips move could make changing for gym class an awkward situation.

I hate my last period. While the high school gods smiled on me for freshman biology, they cursed me with this class. Somehow, I was put in gym with most of the football team. Namely the asshole quarterback, Austin James.

The guy makes it his life's mission to torment me. I spend time working on cars, not working out. I have never been athletic, so they see me as the wimpy outcast. Austin never lets me forget it. He's also the raging douche who dates Sydney and then breaks up with her for somebody else. It's been a cycle for the last two years.

"Hey, grease monkey! You actually going to attempt to not suck today?" Austin yells across the locker room.

Great, he's starting early.

I make my way to my locker to change. I just want to get the last sixty minutes of the school day over with. The sooner that happens, the sooner I can tell Syd the truth. Then she can go to her practice, and I can work on my project in the auto shop.

With my focus elsewhere, I ignore the jokes being made at my expense during the period. While it may be taught that ignoring bullies takes away their power, the opposite is true with Austin. The more I avoid, the more he pushes.

Because I didn't acknowledge any of his jokes during class, he's now standing next to my locker while I change.

"God, you're so small. I bet you need tweezers to jack off." His laugh sounds like nails on a chalkboard. "Your boyfriends must be so disappointed." I glance at him out of the corner of my eye. "You know, 'cause you're gay."

"Not gay, but what does it say about you standing here looking at my junk while I change?" It is one of my rare moments of confidence.

Austin's fist hits my eye before I fully turn towards him. He's got a powerful arm, and I'm knocked to the floor. The room erupts with chants of *"fight, fight fight."* He lands one kick to my ribs before the door bursts open.

The football coach and gym teacher, Mr. Jesip, marches across the tile floor.

"What the hell is going on?" He barks, his voice painfully echoing off the walls.

"Not sure, coach." Austin's hands are up as he plays innocent. "Noah here must have slipped on something."

Mr. Jesip looks down at me, shaking his head. "Noah, if you need to go to the nurse for an ice pack then you can be excused."

With a final disappointed nod, the coach turns around and walks out of the locker room with Austin, discussing his future.

I'm left laying on the cold tile with my head throbbing and ribs bruised. The walk to the nurse's office is slow and painful. An ice pack covers my eye as I sit on a cot until the final bell rings.

Bruises be damned, I have somewhere to be.

I wait anxiously for Sydney by my locker. When she doesn't arrive right away, I head towards her last classroom. The hallway is mostly empty since everyone races out at the end of the day, but I see her standing at the end of the corridor, her back to me. Just as I'm about to call her name, I notice she's not alone.

Austin kneels on the ground in front of her with a sign that says, "Be my prom queen." Sydney bounces up and down on her toes when he stands up.

I turn around as Austin plants a kiss on her perfect lips. He may have assaulted me earlier, but this pain is worse. The football star and the cheerleader are together again. Even though I know he's going to hurt her – again – there is nothing I can do at this moment except walk away.

She'll never be mine.

one

SYDNEY

"And I want balloons, the blue ones with stars, not those silly yellow ones with polka dots."

I can only smile as Tyler plans his fifth birthday party. Even if that smile is fake and conceals the stabbing ache in my chest. He doesn't know a birthday party isn't going to happen this year. The past due notice in my purse is a glaring reminder of my lack of money.

"That all sounds great sweetheart. But if you could only have one thing in the entire world, what would it be?" I glance at him in the rearview mirror. His brown eyes shine with excitement under his faded baseball hat seated perfectly over his brown hair.

"For Daddy to come home and for us to watch baseball," he replies in such a matter-of-fact tone, I can't bear to tell him the truth.

"Well, I'm sure if you ask Daddy, he'll watch baseball with you." Tears threaten to fall as I pull up to his preschool. "In the meantime, you focus on all the amazing things you'll learn in school. Daddy said he's going to pick you up today."

Tyler's little body shakes with excitement as I help him out of the car. What little boy wouldn't be excited his dad, his best friend in the whole world, is coming to see him. I say a silent prayer that he won't be disappointed again.

"Alright, bud, can I have my hug?" I ask, kneeling on the ground.

"Hmmm, ok. But when I'm five, I might be too big for hugs at school."

"We'll see about that." I playfully tug on the brim of his hat before pulling him in for a tight squeeze. "I love you."

"Love you, Mommy."

I watch as he runs to see his classmates. His little backpack bouncing on his shoulders. I long for the days of innocence and optimism. When the worst thing to happen was the wrong kind of jelly on a PB&J.

Climbing back into my ten-year-old car, I hold my breath as I turn the key. It's in need of some maintenance, but I'm trying to stretch it out. It takes two attempts before it starts, shuddering as it idles in the school parking lot.

My drive to work is only five minutes from the school, but the whirlwind of thoughts never stops. Which bill gets paid first? How much is in my savings? What can I give up this month to afford Tyler's birthday present?

At least I don't worry about how I'm going to eat during the week. I have been a waitress at Sal's Diner since I graduated high school. The owner, Sally Hastings, is like a mother to me. I eat for free when I work, and she usually sends me home with food.

Have my son and I grown up on diner food? Yes. Am I grateful for every french fry and grilled cheese? Double yes.

"Good morning, sugar," Louis, our cook, greets me as I walk in.

"Morning, Lou," I reply, pulling my blonde hair into a

ponytail. "Sorry, I'm running behind. I had to drop Tyler at preschool, and the car is acting up."

"No worries, sug, but Sal asked you come to her office this morning."

My stomach drops, and I feel like blood is draining from my body. It's never a good thing to get called into the boss' office first thing in the morning, right? This is the only job I've ever known. My brain goes into overdrive as I try to swallow the lump in my throat.

"Syd." Lou's voice snaps me to reality. "Relax, I think she just wants to check on you and Tyler."

I nod and stare at the closed door in the back of the kitchen. Holding my head up high, I knock twice before opening the door.

"Morning, Sal, you wanted to see me?"

Sally is a robust woman with short black hair and the most beautifully glowing brown skin. "Girl, you look like you saw a ghost. I'm not going to bite you. Take a seat."

I exhale in relief, before taking a seat next to her desk. There isn't a reason for me to feel nervous, I've been in this office a thousand times before. This morning, I'm just extra jumpy and stressed out.

"Sydney, relax, I just want to check in on you. Tyler's birthday is coming up. Are you planning anything?"

"No, not this year. I'll get him a cupcake and a present, but that's all we can do. Austin hasn't—"

"That no good ex-husband of yours is as worthless as shoes on a hog." Sally puts her hand over mine, giving me a gentle squeeze. "Sydney, that man is not worth your tears. Life will sort him out with the trash. Now, I have something for you."

Sal places a white envelope on the desk in front of me. Puzzled, I open it and gasp when I see it's stuffed with cash.

"Sal, I can't take this."

"Hush! You can and will take this money. Consider it a birthday present for Tyler. I expect an invitation to his party on my desk."

"Thank you," I cry, shoving the envelope into my apron pocket. "I better get out there before the regulars get antsy. Thank you again, Sal."

With a pocket full of cash and a shift full of tips, I suddenly feel like things are looking up. The tight feeling in my chest and the unease in my stomach melt away as I start the morning shift, taking and serving breakfast orders.

Feeling slightly more relaxed, the morning rushes by with a sea of hungry diners and the afternoon arrives in a blink of an eye.

I happily get behind the wheel of my car and smile while contemplating what to buy Tyler for his birthday. One thing I know for sure, he's going to get his blue balloon with the stars.

My happy day comes to a grinding halt, along with the engine, as I head home. The sputtering sounds coming from under the hood can't be ignored. Thankfully, a new auto shop nearby either just opened or will open soon.

Please make it. Please let somebody be there.

two
NOAH

"Everything looks good," I say, running my hands along the new work bench.

Even though I'm opening my fourteenth auto shop, I still get the same nervous excitement as I did with my first. Opening this place holds a new level of nervous energy.

It's the first in my hometown—the place I left a year after high school and only visit occasionally. Thank goodness it isn't a small town, less chance of running into certain people.

"Yes, sir. We should be ready for the opening next week. There are just a couple last minute things."

"There always are. I'm sure you'll have it all taken care of. Are you ready for this?"

I look at Thomas—the young man I hired to oversee this location. He's in his early twenties, fresh off the apprenticeship program my garages offer. He showed a level of dedication and maturity beyond his years, which is why I selected him.

"I think so." Thomas scratches the back of his neck.

"Are you sure you want to give the responsibility to somebody like me?"

"Somebody like you?" I square my shoulders to look him in the eyes. "Thomas, you blew all your peers out of the water. You excelled at the things you were taught. Don't think I'm not aware of the extra hours you put in while others in the program partied."

Thomas' eyes finally meet mine, his chest swelling with pride.

"I believe in you and the things you're going to do. This is going to be a big challenge, but I think you'll rise to it. We've set you up with everything you might need, and there are plenty of people to call if you run into issues."

"Thank you, Mr. Reed. I will do my best to not let you down."

"Thomas, please call me Noah. I may own the place, but I hate feeling like a stuffy suit."

Thomas chuckles, "I suppose that explains the old pickup truck and blue jeans."

"Comfort and style, kid. It's the only way to live life." I huff out a laugh as we make our way towards the exit. "Now what else—"

The sputtering of a car engine cuts me off as a small sedan pulls into the parking lot. Thomas and I exchange looks. There is nothing promising about the death rattles as it inches to a stop.

"I guess I should tell them we aren't open for business yet." Thomas looks to me for guidance as if he's worried about making the wrong choice.

"You could. Or we can talk to them about the issues they're having with the car. Maybe set them up as your first appointment."

"Oh! I didn't even think about that." Thomas sheepishly toes a small rock on the ground.

"It will come to you, Thomas. With time."

I follow him to the sedan, allowing him to take the lead. I may own the company, but he runs this shop. He reaches for the door handle as the driver's door opens. My faith in him only grows bigger as he offers his hand to help the woman out of the car.

At the sight of her, my heart crashes to the ground and my stomach flips. Beads of sweat form on my back. Sydney Parker stands in the parking lot of my new shop. How is it possible she looks better now than high school? She was perfect back then.

I stand motionless as Thomas talks to her. My lungs forget their purpose the moment her eyes meet mine. Her lips part as those beautiful blue pools stare at me.

"Noah?"

Hearing her voice for the first time in ten years does something to my soul. I'm instantly transported back to high school, madly in love with a girl.

"Hey, Syd," I manage to croak over the dryness in my throat.

"Oh my God. NOAH!" Sydney's smile lights up as she wraps me in a hug.

My arms wrap around her with ease, like it's something they have always done, instead of always wishing they could. She still smells like strawberries.

Pulling back, she narrows her eyes at me. "Noah Reed, where have you been?" She smacks my chest before looking at me with wide eyes. "I-I-I'm sorry. I just can't believe you're here."

Thomas clears his throat, reminding me of his presence—and that other people exist in the world.

Sydney steps back, tucking a lock of hair behind her ear. Is she blushing?

Fuck me, she is blushing. I mentally pat myself on the back for her adorable rosy cheeks.

"We haven't officially opened yet, ma'am. But I could get you scheduled for an appointment." Thomas' voice shakes a bit.

"Oh." I watch Sydney swallow hard. "I hate to ask but is there another shop nearby that could help me today?"

"Oh umm—" Thomas starts.

"Come on, boss. It wouldn't hurt us to at least look under the hood." I give him a reassuring nod before looking at Sydney. "Thomas runs this place."

"Are you a mechanic here?" she asks, looking me up and down.

"I'm here to help things get started until the full-time crew comes on."

I'm lying my ass off because as far as I know nobody here knows what I do. I was the outcast in school so nobody followed my success afterwards. Which is fine because I didn't have to deal with people pretending they care in order to be friends with the rich guy. This may be my fourteenth auto shop, but I own the entire parent company of Jensen Automotive. Named for my grandfather, Jensen Reed, who bought me my first wrench.

It's not an accident I've avoided opening a location here. There's a reason I left after high school and didn't look back. Right now, part of that reason is standing in front of me.

"Ma'am, if you wouldn't mind popping the hood." Thomas is all manners and professionalism. This kid is the right choice.

Sydney reaches into her car and pulls the hood latch. As Thomas and I start to survey the damage, she steps away to take a phone call.

Glancing up from the almost dead engine, I notice her

posture and demeanor have changed. Something else is wrong. I step towards her out of instinct, protecting her was always my goal in school.

"Yes, I understand. No, I'm so sorry there was a pickup person arranged for him. I will be there as soon as possible. Again, I am so sorry." She pushes end on her call before running a hand through her hair.

"Everything ok?" I cautiously ask, stepping closer.

"Um, no. I need to pick up my son at preschool." She looks over my shoulder at her car. "Is it safe to drive?"

Thomas shuts the hood and wipes his hands on the rag in his pocket. "I'm sorry, ma'am, but no. At minimum you need an oil change, but I'm sure we'll find more issues after a closer look."

Sydney's eyes well with tears. "That bad? Um, ok. I have to, um, call a c—"

"Sydney." My voice is soft as I put a hand on her shoulder. "Let me drive you to pick up your son."

"Oh no, I couldn't let you do that."

"It's no trouble. I'll drop you two off at your place and come back to finish looking at your car."

Sydney's shoulders relax as she slowly nods. "Thank you."

Grabbing the car seat from her car, I secure it in the middle of my truck's bench seat. This classic old girl wasn't restored to be a family vehicle, but a small part of me doesn't hate seeing a child seat inside.

We pull out of the parking lot, and Sydney is already making a call. Her cheeks are red, and her eyes hold a murderous glare.

"Austin! You were supposed to pick up Tyler from preschool," she yells into the phone. "What do you mean something came up? What the hell is more important than your son? You know what? Never mind, I already know." She ends the call, tossing the cell phone into her purse.

"Austin? As in Austin James?" I try not to roll my eyes.

"One in the same." Sydney blows out a breath of air.

"So you guys are—"

"Divorced." Sydney turns to face me, and I see the dark circles for the first time. The exhaustion in her eyes. "For about a year."

"I'm sorry to hear that."

She doesn't respond, only huffs out a breath and looks out the window. "The preschool is on Juniper Street."

"Ok."

We don't say anything else for the rest of the short drive. The preschool has been there since before I can remember. It's not lost on me that while I was living an entirely different life, she was still here. Sydney, the girl who wanted to see the world, was still in the same neighborhood, taking her son to the same preschool she went to.

"Thank you for doing this. I can pay you some gas money." Sydney's voice cuts through my thoughts.

"I'm happy to help. And no, you will not give me gas money."

I think she's going to argue when she opens and closes her mouth several times before gently smiling. Relief shows in her eyes. What has that asshole Austin done to her?

What happened to my beautiful, lively Sydney?

SYDNEY

I AM GOING TO KILL AUSTIN. I'M NOT JUST GOING TO YELL at him. He deserves worse than being told how much he sucks. No, I may actually kill him and drag his body to the middle of nowhere to burn it.

It's one thing to let me down. He's been doing it for years, and I'm immune to the stupid excuses at this point. But breaking our son's heart over and over has me seeing red.

Tyler sits at a little table in his classroom, playing with some toy cars. His saint of a teacher has stayed late to make sure he has a safe place.

My heart hurts. How could somebody who isn't related to him care more about his well-being than his actual father?

His teacher sees me first and motions for me to step into the hall.

"Ms. Avery, I'm so sorry," I apologize profusely. "I know it's not ok, and I will make sure this never happens again."

"Mrs. James, you're right. It's not ok he wasn't picked up on time."

My heart sinks to the floor. I'm failing as a mother, and his teacher makes sure I know it.

"Tyler was very excited all day. He told everyone that his father was going to pick him up."

"Yes, ma'am." I stand with my gaze fixed to the floor, accepting her obvious disappointment.

"Then it seems to me the apology should be coming from him not you." I glance up at her with surprise. "Sydney, you are an amazing mother. Tyler is smart, bright, happy, and thriving. So please don't apologize for the thoughtlessness of his father."

The hot sting of tears blurs my vision as I nod. For the last year, Austin's family has blamed me for the divorce. At times, I felt the entire world saw me as the bad person for ending our marriage. I didn't realize how much of that I had been carrying around until this moment.

"We have a policy of charging for afterschool care when a child is not picked up. But I'm going to waive that this time." Ms. Avery gives me a soft smile and a wink. "I have a good for nothing ex-husband, too."

Tyler is still happily playing with the toy cars when I walk into this classroom. But he isn't alone because sitting cross-legged on the floor is Noah Reed.

My Noah.

Well, he was never *my* Noah. But he was the one person who made high school feel like a dream instead of a chore. There was no pressure to be anything other than myself with him. I didn't have to be the popular cheerleader or the honor student.

The hours we spent studying in the library were an excuse for me to cut loose and relax. Noah made me laugh and enjoyed my silly antics. He let me talk for hours about my outlandish high school dreams.

Too many romance books and princess stories. That's what others said, especially Austin. I suppose that should have been a sign. But we were the cheerleader and quarterback love story that everyone expected.

Even me at one time.

But Noah Reed was the outcast, not a bad boy, but not a popular kid. He was kind, smart, funny, and never let me doubt myself or my dreams. At some point, that all changed, and I don't know what I did to push him away.

Just before prom he became distant and suddenly didn't have time to hang out or talk. It felt like a door had slammed between us. Perhaps I didn't take enough time to search for the key.

"Mommy!" Tyler's excited little voice soothes my soul. "This is Noah, we're playing cars. Here, you can be the red car. I don't have a pink one for you."

"Oh, baby, that's ok. We need to head home anyway. Can you say thank you to Ms. Avery for hanging out with you?"

"Thank you, Ms. Avery." He repeats in the same schoolhouse cadence every child has.

With an appreciative nod, I usher Tyler outside to Noah's truck. He loves all things automobile and is more than happy to jump into a pickup truck. I watch as Noah lets him play with the steering wheel before buckling him into his car seat.

The ride home is mostly filled with Tyler talking about his day and Noah and I listening quietly and occasionally sharing a smile. I feel a strange peacefulness, sitting in the old pickup and watching my son's little hands wildly gesture, as Noah happily drives us home.

"Mommy?" Tyler's voice cuts through my thoughts. "Why didn't Daddy pick me up? You said he was coming today. Was I bad?"

My eyes widen with shock, sadness, and anger. How could my innocent boy think he did anything wrong? Let alone anything bad enough his father wouldn't be there for him?

"You absolutely were not bad." I reach over for his little hand and squeeze it in mine. "Daddy...he just...well he—I don't know why he wasn't there, sweetie. We can call him tonight so you can tell him all about your day."

Thankfully, Noah pulls up to the house and I don't need to make more excuses, which has been my primary job with Austin. Even before we had Tyler.

Noah helps Tyler out of the truck and carries the car seat to my front porch. I'm suddenly embarrassed at the mess inside as Noah stands in the doorway.

I always had a crush on him in school because there was something different about him.

And now? He seems so put together and mature. Not to mention insanely handsome with his defined biceps and cut-from-stone jawline.

"Thank you so much for the help. Are you sure I can't give you a little gas money?"

"I'm not taking your money, poppy."

Noah gave me the nickname in school after I told him they were my favorite flower.

"You remembered." I feel my cheeks grow hot and my stomach flip.

"Of course, I remember." His voice is low and a little gravelly. His hazel eyes study me in a way that he hasn't before.

"Noah, come see my cars and trucks." Tyler calls from inside. "Mommy, can Noah stay for dinner?"

For a moment, I think he's going to say he needs to leave, but instead, he just raises an eyebrow. A sly smile crossing his lips. Who could resist that smile?

"Do you like dino nuggets?"

four
NOAH

"This is my favorite." Tyler happily holds up a red car.

It's easy to tell because there isn't a scratch on it. All the other cars have been played with outside or have crayon markings. But this one looks brand new out of the box. An impressive thing for a four-year-old.

"That's a Chevy Camaro SS. A really awesome car." I smile to myself. It's my favorite car, too. I started restoring one myself, opting for black with a red pinstripe.

"You know lots about cars." He says setting the car down gently.

"Yeah, I do. I've always loved cars. I started fixing them when I wasn't much older than you. I used to help my grandpa in his garage."

"Wow."

"Dinner's ready," Sydney announces, setting a pitcher of water on the table. "Wash your hands."

Tyler moans a little at the idea, but we take turns using the same kitchen sink. I glance around the combined area of the kitchen and dining room as I dry my hands with a dish towel. A small wooden table with four chairs sits in one corner, and crayon drawings cover the refrigerator.

The stack of mail on the counter catches my eye. I take a quick peek at the top envelope with a glaring red "past due" stamp. A subtle glance around shows me a few areas in need of repairs.

I pull out Sydney's seat before taking mine. She's already plated our dinners with nuggets, macaroni and cheese, and carrot sticks. Her plate makes me pause because Tyler and I have a pile of food while she took whatever was left over.

"I'm not that hungry," she explains when she catches me eyeing her plate. "Please eat."

Without hesitation, I scrape half the food on my plate onto hers. Before she can protest, I shake my head because this isn't an argument she would win. But I'm also not going to argue in front of her son. It's clear from his clean bedroom, well maintained clothes, and healthy dinner that she is shielding him from how much she's struggling.

I grew up with poor parents; I know what pinching every penny looks like. Sydney is squeezing hers with every ounce of strength she has.

After dinner, I help clean things up while Tyler happily watches cartoons. We don't say much as we wash dishes in her tiny kitchen. Before long it's time for me to leave, and I'm left with a longing for any excuse to stay.

"It was so good to see you. Thank you again,"

"Anytime. I'll look at your car tomorrow—"

"Oh my God, my car." Her voice goes from relaxed to frantic. "I forgot I don't have a car. How am I going to get to work? Or take Tyler to school?"

Without thinking, I pull her into my arms. The smell of her strawberry shampoo fills my nose. "Relax, poppy, I can give you both a ride tomorrow. If we can't figure out the issue with your car, then I'll pick you up."

"But the shop isn't open yet, I can't afford a tow truck or even repairs." She starts to tremble. "It's such a mess, and now I'm crying all over your shirt. Will your boss let you work in the shop if it's not open?"

"I think he'll be fine with it." I step back to look her in the eye. "We'll get it sorted out."

She wipes a tear from the corner of her eye as she nods. "Thank you, Noah."

I make sure she's inside and the door is locked before leaving. Once I'm in my truck, I make a call.

"Good evening, Mr. Reed. What can I do for you?"

My assistant, Felicia, is used to phone calls at any time of day. She's never failed at managing the tasks I give her. I'm not some unreasonable boss. But there are times I need results quickly, and she is the person I trust to make it happen.

"I want everything you can get on Austin James, by tomorrow morning."

"Of course, sir."

I hit 'end' on the call, tossing my phone on the bench seat. There's no reason for me to get involved. I haven't seen Sydney in over ten years. But it's not just Sydney. Tyler is the innocent one in this entire mess. For his father to not show up for him is inexcusable.

Worst yet, he's left them to barely scrape by. I'm sure the one past due notice I saw on the counter isn't the only one. Sydney is driving an old car that barely runs and her once lively eyes are shadowed with exhaustion and worry.

My mind goes back to the days of studying together. Her laughter filled the otherwise quiet library. We would split a coke and bag of chips—always barbecue flavor because regular potato chips were too boring.

Life seems simple now when I look back on it.

Although, if you had asked me then, it was the most complicated and confusing time in my life. I was in love with a girl who was too good for me. But she never acted like it. Instead, she offered me kindness and friendship, even if the others in her circle thought I was nothing.

The drive to my parent's house doesn't take long.

They still live in the area, but in a new place I bought them a couple of years ago. Three thousand square feet with two acres of land extending into the nearby woods. It's larger than they need for just the two of them. But, it gives me a place to stay and work when I'm here with enough privacy for me to not intrude on them.

After decades of scraping by on my father's wages as a plumber, they now don't have to worry about anything. Dad is semi-retired and mom happily spends afternoons in her dream garden.

"Hi, honey." Mom has greeted me the same way my entire life. "Are you hungry? You missed dinner."

"I'm good," I say, kicking off my boots by the back door.

"How are things at the new shop?" She asks, standing at the large farmhouse sink in the kitchen.

I made sure every inch of this house was what my parents always dreamed of. For mom, that was a big kitchen. Her request was white cabinets and stone counters with pale yellow walls. She said it reminds her of fresh butter.

"Everything looks great, and the opening is on schedule for next week."

"Which means you'll be leaving then, I suppose." Mom's soft blue eyes land on her feet.

"Let's not worry about when I'm leaving right now." I say with a kiss on the top of her head. At five foot three she's been shorter than me since middle school. "Do you remember Sydney Parker?"

Her eyes narrow in thought. "That sweet girl you were friends with in school?"

"That's her." My lips curve into a smile as I think about Sydney. "I ran into her today at the shop. Her car broke down in the parking lot."

"Well, that's nice. Not about her car of course but seeing an old friend. How is she?"

The earlier warmth in my chest chills as I think about her current situation. "She's a mother. Divorced and the ex is a real piece of work. It doesn't look like he helps a whole lot."

"Such a shame." My mom's shoulder length hair swishes as she shakes her head. The silver streaks are starting to outnumber the natural brown. "I remember you always talking fondly of her. I hope you two have a chance to catch up while you're in town."

Patting my back gently, mom walks out of the kitchen and leaves me with my thoughts. One thing continues to play over and over in my mind—the way her eyes lit up when I called her "poppy".

NOAH

Ten years ago

"NOAH? ARE YOU IN HERE?" SYDNEY'S WHITE CHEER shoes look out of place in the grease-filled auto shop.

"I'm in the pit," I yell, turning the wrench over my head.

I've been working part time in my grandfather's auto shop for a couple of years. I mostly do oil changes, but it's good practice and lets me turn wrenches.

Sydney crouches down to look under the car I'm working on. Her cheer skirt rides dangerously high on her legs. It takes everything in me not to steal a peek underneath.

"Can I come down?"

"No way. You'll get grease all over your cheer stuff. I'll be done in a minute."

Five minutes later, I climbed out of the pit and wipe my hands on a shop towel. Sydney is sitting on a bench outside, her eyes closed, as she enjoys the afternoon sun. I could look at her like this forever.

"That was the longest minute in history," she teases when she finally notices me.

"Sorry, but good work takes time." I hold out a bag of barbecue potato chips for us to share.

She pats the bench next to her, inviting me to sit, as she tears open the bag. I make sure to keep some distance, so I don't get her uniform dirty.

"Have you figured out who you're asking to prom?" she asks as the toes of her shoes kick at the ground.

"Nope. Prom's not my kind of thing." I'm lying. I have been planning to ask her for months. Every dime I've earned has been going towards the event—the tuxedo, tickets, dinner, and even a limo ride.

"Come on, Noah. It's senior year, and prom is supposed to be one of those magical memories to cherish."

"For people like you, maybe. Not for the guy nobody worries about."

"I worry about you." She meets my eyes, and for a moment, there is something different. But she blinks it away before I can figure it out. "I'm going dress shopping tomorrow."

"Have you decided who you're going to go with? I'm sure you have several choices."

"There is somebody I hope to go with. In fact, I dreamed about it the other night."

"Oh, really?" I cock my head at her.

"Yup, I saw the whole thing. My dress, his tux, and even the corsage of poppies."

"Poppies?" I know they're her favorite, but I want her to keep talking.

"Mmmhmm." She nods, happily popping a chip in her mouth. "Poppies and roses with baby's breath." Sydney's eyes look at her shoes for a moment before she looks at me again. "Poppies are my favorite. They close at night to protect themselves from the cold but then open again in the morning sun to show their beauty."

For a moment, it feels like we're alone. There isn't a sound in the world. I tuck a strand of hair behind her ear as the sun shines on Sydney's face. Her full beauty on display in the warm light.

"Noah, I—"

The blaring car horn and loud music startle both of us.

"Hey, Syd, need a ride to practice?"

Austin James smirks at me from behind the wheel of his new Honda Civic, a birthday present from his parents. The kid has never earned anything in his life, a fact he happily flaunts.

"I should go," she whispers, looking at Austin's car. "I don't want him to make a scene."

"Sure." I slide away from her on the bench.

"I'll see you tomorrow?"

"See you tomorrow, poppy."

Sydney's smile is brighter than the afternoon sun. There's a slight blush to her cheeks as she bites her lip. She's barely in the car when Austin grabs the chips from her hand.

"Gross, barbecue." He chucks the bag out the window into the parking lot. "You look hot in the uniform, Syd."

Just like her favorite flower, I watch her brightness close as Austin pulls away, shielding the real her from his prying eyes.

He'll never see her beauty like I do.

SYDNEY

True to his word, Noah arrives first thing in the morning to pick us up. Again, not willing to take any gas money for his troubles.

Without thinking about it I find myself staring at him as we drive towards the diner. The fabric of a dark blue Henley stretches over his biceps. His dark hair is short on the sides and longer on top, giving it kind of a messy look and his perfectly trimmed stubble begs to be brushed against my skin. The worn jeans and work boots complete the sexiest workingman look on the planet.

Noah Reed is incredibly hot.

"What? Did I miss a spot shaving?" He asks, scrubbing a hand over his chiseled jaw.

"You look different and the same all at once."

"Is that a bad thing?" He glances over at me.

"No. I just can't believe you're here after all this time. What have you been doing? Where did you go?"

Noah shifts in his seat, as if he doesn't want to tell me. I suppose he has a right to keep his personal life to himself. We haven't talked in so long, it's partially my fault.

Austin and I started dating again when he asked me to the prom. My friendship with Noah seemed to fade for the rest of senior year. We didn't see each other very much after graduation, and he moved away before summer was over.

"I worked at my grandpa's shop for a while, then took an apprenticeship out of state." He hasn't looked at me once. "What about you? How was college?"

"Oh it, well I…" I can't bring myself to tell him the truth. Thankfully we pull up to the diner before I can finish. "If you won't take gas money then how about breakfast? We have the best in town."

Noah studies the diner for a moment before turning his gaze to me. "How on earth could you top dino nuggets?"

"You can't, but Lou, our cook, can sure try." I give him a little wink before getting out of his truck.

We're both still laughing when I spot Austin standing near the entrance. It doesn't take him long to lock eyes with me and come storming across the parking lot.

"Syd, I need to talk to you." He looks like he hasn't slept.

"I need to get to work," I grit, stepping around him.

Austin grabs my arm, his fingers digging into my skin, as he pulls me close to him. The smell of stale beer and whiskey on his breath makes me feel sick. Before I can protest, Noah steps between us.

"I wouldn't grab her like that," he says, grabbing Austin's wrist.

Brief shock crosses Austin's face, then he focuses on Noah's features. His chuckle isn't a friendly as he sneers. "Noah fucking Reed. Know your place, shithead. I'm talking to my wife."

"Ex-wife," Noah corrects, stepping in closer. His voice

is low, edging on dangerous. "My place is right here between you and her. Now let her go."

"Fucking prick," Austin mumbles before grudgingly releasing my arm. "Look, Syd, I really do need to talk to you."

It feels like an eternity as the three of us stand there, before Noah's eyes meet mine. I offer him a small nod, knowing he would happily punch Austin right now if I asked him.

"I'll be standing right over there." Noah glowers at my ex-husband and points to the entrance. When he turns to me, there is still an edge of danger in his stare, but his voice softens. "Are you ok to be with him?"

Why is my stomach full of butterflies? And not the nervous kind.

"It's ok. I'll just be a minute."

With one last death stare, Noah nods as I step into the parking lot to deal with Austin.

"You fucking him now?" Austin snaps, "you don't take long."

"Jesus, Austin," I inhale, fighting the urge to punch his smug face myself. He would love nothing more than to bait me into losing my temper. "First of all, anyone I may be seeing or fucking is none of your business. Secondly, Noah is a good friend who helped me when you flaked on *our son* yesterday."

"I told you something came up." His tone is clipped and harsh. "Look, I need some money."

The laugh is out of me before I can suppress it. "You need money? You? Need money?" All thoughts of staying calm and having a rational conversation are gone. Never once in his selfish, pampered life has Austin thought of anyone but himself. I lived with that for too long. "Well, you're barking up the wrong fucking tree. I'm raising OUR son, working my ass off to keep the bills paid. The bills *you* skipped out on. *I* need money, Austin!"

"Damn it, Syd." Austin steps closer to me, lowering his voice. "I owe people money, and they want it soon."

"What?" The shock snaps me out of my previous bout of laughter. "Austin, what the hell did you get mixed up in?"

"Look, can I get the money or not?"

I am suddenly too aware of his fidgeting hands and unfocused eyes. "Are you high? I'm not asking because of the money thing. Are you actually high right now?"

"Fucking forget it. Thanks for being a selfish bitch."

Austin turns around and storms off towards his car. I can't help but find it funny how he needs money yet drives a nicer car than I do. He didn't need to get a ride here today. He drove his fully functioning less-than-a-decade-old car.

My cheeks are red with anger. He's got some balls coming to my place of work and asking for money. As the person who used to sleep with him, I know what he's really working with. So, desperation must be the only other explanation.

"Everything alright?" Noah asks, opening the diner door for me. He presses his hand against the middle of my back as I step inside.

His touch is like a cozy blanket on a winter morning. Warm, comforting, and something I wouldn't mind wrapping up in.

"Yeah, fine. Just Austin being…well himself." I shrug out of my coat and tuck my purse under the counter. "No need to let him spoil breakfast. Now what can I get you?"

Noah's smile melts away the last five minutes. His eyes sparkle as he looks at me. "What do you recommend?"

"The mixed berry french toast is my favorite. Tyler prefers the silver dollar pancakes."

"I'll take the pancakes."

"Siding with the kid." I nod with a playful smile. "Alright, I know where your loyalty is."

His deep laughter sends a tingle through my body. After putting in his order, I pour him a cup of coffee and head to my other customers. All the while, I can feel his eyes watching me. Sure enough, when I grab his order from the kitchen window, Noah's eyes are locked on me.

"Breakfast is served." I smile nervously, setting down the plate of pancakes. Just like I do with Tyler's breakfast I made a smiley face out of whipped cream and fruit.

My heart flutters when Noah looks up from his plate and winks.

Yeah, Noah Reed is hot.

seven

NOAH

AFTER MY SOMEWHAT KID-LIKE BREAKFAST, I TUCK A generous tip under my plate and leave the diner. Sydney insisted the meal was on the house, but that doesn't mean I can't tip a good waitress.

Especially one as breathtaking as her. I couldn't stop watching the swing of her hips as she moved from table to table. If high school Sydney was my dream girl, grown up Sydney is my dirty fantasy.

I pull into the parking lot of the new shop noticing that Sydney's car isn't there. The moment of panic is eased when I see it inside behind the glass roll up door.

"Hey, boss, I pushed it inside last night so it wouldn't be left in the parking lot," Thomas greets me at the door.

"Good thinking. Have you looked under the hood this morning?"

"No, I got here a few minutes ago. I could now if you want."

"Nah, I'll look at the car. You deal with whatever you had planned. I appreciate your help and discretion yesterday."

He didn't have to cover for me and easily could have outed me as being his boss. Thomas nods in understanding and heads to his office.

Of all the places I have traveled and things I have done, nothing beats turning wrenches. I have this place all to myself and it's exactly how I want it. There are no distractions from business meetings or phone calls from suppliers. Just me, an engine in need of repair and all the tools I could want.

After poking around for about an hour, the list of repairs is adding up fast. I know that Sydney can't afford half of what this car needs. I'm contemplating what to do about it when my phone rings.

"This is Noah."

"Good morning, sir. I have the information you requested on Austin James." Felicia is all business as usual. Although I envision her leaning casually in her desk chair as if this task were too easy.

When I travel, she runs the office for me. Nobody messes with Felicia.

"What did you find out?" I set down the wrench in my hand.

"I had to call in a favor on this one. So, you owe me a bottle of something expensive."

"Done."

Felicia has a passion for good bourbon, fine cigars, and curvy brunettes. She sees more women than I do. Her reach into the world of personal information is something I don't ask questions about. She's more than a personal assistant, she's my private investigator as well.

I didn't build an empire without making a few enemies. Too many people want something for nothing when you're rich. Everyone in my life is run through Felicia.

"It would have been easier if you told me that you were friends with the guy."

"Friends is a stretch. We went to high school together, that's all."

I feel her rolling her eyes as she clears her throat. "Austin James, divorced with one child. The guy has bounced between jobs since college. Never lasting more than… well, the longest was eighteen months. Two months ago, he was fired from his job at a sporting goods store. Looks like he lives on unemployment and a monthly deposit from his parents."

"He's getting an allowance from mommy and daddy?"

"I think they pay his rent, it's the same amount every month." There's a rustling sound on the phone, and Felicia's voice is muffled. "Sorry about that. Somebody thought they could see you without an appointment."

"Anyone I need to talk to?"

"Are you interested in switching where you buy office supplies?"

"Am I interested in that?" I ask, knowing the answer.

"You are not. Now if I can finish before I'm late for my brunch date?" Felicia clears her throat again. "Aside from being a grade-A douche. He's also in debt and not just to the credit card company and bank. Seems Mr. James has a gambling problem."

My jaw tightens as I listen. That fucker has wasted his life and now has gambling debts. I'm willing to bet he showed up this morning asking Sydney for money.

"In addition, there is a drinking problem and possibly a recent switch to drugs."

"Who does he owe and how much?"

"That's going to take me some more time."

"Find out." Before hanging up, I add, "Felicia, buy yourself two bottles of bourbon."

"Already ordered."

She hangs up without another word. I'm not sure what I'm going to do with this new information. But I like to be prepared for things. I knew what a fucking idiot Austin was in school, but this is a whole new level, even for him.

My fists clench at my sides. I should have punched him this morning when he grabbed Sydney.

Distracting myself with her car, the morning melts into the afternoon. I knock out some of the smaller things on the repair list. She doesn't need to know about those.

"Thomas," I say, rapping my knuckles on his office door. "I'll be working on the car myself. Don't worry about any of the supplies, they won't come from your stock or budget. But I am going to leave it here for now."

"Sure."

I don't need to ask for his permission, and we both know it. But it's a courtesy and a show of respect to let him know what's happening.

It's time to pick up Sydney from work before getting Tyler from school. I'm going to have to tell her about the car, and my stomach is in knots. Yes, I could easily handle the repairs and not say a word to her. But she still doesn't know my secret.

"I should just tell her," I tell myself during the drive. "Stop being a baby about this. Just look her in the eye and tell her."

I step inside the diner and don't see Sydney anywhere. I grab a seat at the counter to wait for her when a heavyset woman comes from the back.

"Hey, sugar, what can I get you?"

"Nothing for me. I'm just waiting for Sydney."

I watch her lips press together as she gives me a thorough up and down. She's judging me. "You Noah?"

"Yes, ma'am." I swallow hard, suddenly nervous.

"Sally Hastings. I own this joint." Sally offers her well-manicured hand to me. "Everyone calls me Sal."

"Pleasure to meet you, Sal." My shoulders relax as we shake hands. "How's business been today? Any unwanted visitors?"

Sal eyes me with a questioning stare. "Unwanted, like say, a good for nothing ex-husband?"

"You're not a fan of Austin?"

"I'd be his number one fan if he was a speed bump on the highway."

I chuckle while thinking of Sal driving down the highway at full speed with Austin in her sights. Her hating Austin means she'll have Sydney's back if he showed at the diner again. Putting Sally Hastings on my list of allies.

"Sydney's in the alley. Come with me, I'll show you."

Confused, I follow Sal through the kitchen and out the back door. For an alley behind a diner, it's rather clean. There is a mural of two hands clasped together surrounded by flowers on the brick wall. The words "Helping Hands Soup Kitchen" painted in bright paint underneath.

At the end of the alley, Sydney stands behind a folding table lined with a large pot of soup and prepackaged sandwiches.

"She started this on her own a couple years ago," Sal tells me as I watch from the doorway. "Took her own money and bought all the food. She only asked me to use the kitchen for food prep. Came in early, stayed late so she wasn't working on the clock."

"Sydney feeds the homeless with her own money?" I ask, shaking my head.

Her blonde hair swirls around her face in the breeze as she smiles at the people lining up in front of her.

"She did at first. But once that good for nothing ex of hers skipped out, I started picking up the tab."

"You're a good person, Sal."

"I'm a good businesswoman, who can write off the expenses. But Sydney does this from her heart." Sal chuckles before turning her honey-colored eyes on me. "That girl has been through hell. See to it that I don't have to add you to my bad list."

"I promise, Sal," I say, turning my eyes toward Sydney. "She's safe with me."

eight
SYDNEY

THERE IS SOMETHING ABOUT NOAH'S PRESENCE THAT STIRS butterflies in my stomach. Whenever he's near me, there is a feeling of calm and a tingle of excitement. The shiver that ran up my spine a moment ago is how I know he's there. He and Sal are in a deep conversation when I glance up, but those eyes are focused on me.

He observes for a while before offering to help. Side by side, we spend the next hour serving meals to those who need it. Just when I think he couldn't be any sexier, he carries all the supplies back inside for me.

"All set?" he asks after setting the soup pot in the sink.

"Almost," I say, glancing at the packaged meal in my hand. "I need to take a little walk."

Noah follows me as I walk the four blocks to my destination, a small shack behind the overpass. Well, it's a pieced together shelter made of tarps, wood, plastic bags, and anything else that could be salvaged.

"George, are you here?" I yell, knocking on the side of the lean-to. "It's fine, promise," I whisper, giving Noah a little nudge.

He's looking at where we are with both confusion and perhaps a little apprehension. Before he can ask me anything, we're interrupted by a gravelly cough.

"Who's there?" George barks between hacking coughs.

"Room service."

There's rustling inside before the tarp flap opens. George, with his long shaggy hair and beard, squints against the afternoon sun. He's only been to the soup kitchen once, but I make sure he always gets a meal.

Nodding his head in appreciation, George takes the offered meal and shuts us out.

Noah doesn't say anything until we're almost to the diner. "He was pleasant."

"George has been homeless for two decades. He doesn't ask for help, and it took me six months for him to finally accept a meal."

"Why?"

"He's stubborn and proud."

"No, I mean why keep trying?"

I stop walking to look at him. "Because everyone, no matter their story, deserves a hot meal and to feel like somebody in the world is thinking about them."

Noah steps closer and tucks my hair behind my ear. "You're a remarkable woman."

Without realizing, I've stepped closer to him and pressed my cheek into his hand. Before I can think, Noah presses his lips to mine. It's innocent, soft, and over far too soon.

"What was that for?" I whisper.

"To thank you for adding good into the world."

The earlier butterflies I felt are nothing compared to the swirling vortex his kiss stirred inside me. Shyly, I bite my lower lip savoring the moment, still tasting his lips on mine.

Say something to him, Sydney.

"We need to pick up Tyler."

That was all you could think of?

Noah walks me to his truck, opening the door to help me inside. He doesn't hold my hand or pull me close to him. I'm left to wonder if the kiss was innocent or if he's holding back.

We don't speak until he drops Tyler and I off at home. He carries the car seat inside and sets it by the coat rack.

Tyler runs off to his room to play, leaving us to stand there alone.

"Syd, about your car," he says, rubbing the back of his neck. "It needs a lot of work."

"I know. I expected it to be bad." Those all too familiar tears start to sting my eyes again. "I can't afford repairs. Maybe I should just sell it to a junkyard. They pay for cars, right?"

My mind spins in overdrive before remembering the money Sal gave me. It's still tucked inside my apron. Reaching into the pocket I take the envelope and hand it to Noah.

"Sal gave me a bonus. She told me to use it for Tyler's birthday next week."

"Syd, I—" Noah's phone rings before he can finish. Looking at the screen, his eyebrows draw together. "I'm sorry, I need to take this."

"Of course. Thank you again for everything."

Noah leans in to kiss my cheek, "We'll finish talking about your car later. Keep the money."

Before I can argue, he puts the envelope in my apron pocket and leaves. He presses his phone to his ear the moment he's outside. Even walking away from me, I can see the tension in his back.

"Mama?" Tyler's little voice startles me.

"Oh goodness, sweetheart." I reach over and tickle his side with a smile. "I didn't even hear you walking down the hall. Are you in ninja mode?"

"No," he whispers, his little eyes focused down at his shoes. He didn't even smile at being tickled or from being compared to a ninja.

"What's the matter?" I ask, kneeling on the floor in front of him.

"You can have this," Tyler whispers, showing me the tiny piggy bank in his hand.

I bought it when he was a baby and occasionally put in a quarter. My silly thought was the spare change would add up for Tyler to use when he was eighteen. It's been a long time since I put anything into it.

"Baby, why are you giving me your piggy bank?"

Tyler's sweet little face is red as he holds back the giant tears in his eyes. I know why he's giving it to me. My baby boy knows that things are tough.

Sitting on the floor, I pull him into my arms, cradling him like I used to when he was a baby. "I am the luckiest mommy in the history of mommies. You keep your piggy bank, Tyler. Thank you for offering, and I love you so much for being the kindest boy ever."

Tyler may have physical features like his father, but he has my heart. Which I am so thankful for. My boy is going to be a kind and caring man one day.

I don't know how life spiraled this way. When Austin and I got married it seemed like everything fell into place. Now I'm sitting on the floor of a house I'm on the verge of losing, telling my four-year-old to keep his money.

What am I going to do now? Maybe I can get a small loan from the bank. Surely that's what personal loans are for.

After Tyler's bath and bedtime stories, I sit down at the

kitchen table to look at finances. The stack of bills on the table seems to have grown. One by one, I look at the amount due before deciding which ones I can pay this month.

It's almost ten by the time I pull myself away from the nightmare that are my finances. Tomorrow, I'm going to ask for extra shifts at the diner. On my next day off, I'll go to the bank to discuss a personal loan.

nine
SYDNEY

Four years and nine months ago

My stomach flutters as I wait for Austin to come home. Is it possible to feel movement already? I'll have to look it up. There is no way I can sit still right now. Not after I took a pregnancy test this afternoon and saw the word *PREGNANT*.

We've talked about it a few times over the last couple of years, but the timing never seemed right. Truth be told, the timing right now might not be right either. Austin only just started his new job, and we've been fighting.

I know having a baby won't fix things, but maybe it will help us be close again. Truth be told, I haven't been on the pill for a long time, but nothing ever happened. This must be a sign the universe feels it's my time to be a mother.

My hands have been over my belly all afternoon. I'm not showing, but I can't help but touch the spot where my precious little one is growing.

"You are going to be so loved little one." I talk to where my hand is placed. "I know your daddy is going to want to teach you all about sports even if you have no interest in them. I am always going to be around no matter what even if you don't like sports, which is ok with me."

I check the clock on the stove one more time. Austin should have been home by now. Maybe things were busy. I splurged all my saved-up tip money from this week to make his favorite dinner. The little box on the table has the test inside with a baby jersey.

My mind wanders to all those precious online videos of women surprising their husbands with the news. I wonder if he'll laugh or cry. Maybe he'll scoop me up in his arms and tell me he loves me. It's been a while since he's said that.

ME

> Hey babe, dinner is staying warm in the oven. Will you be home soon?

Feeling tired after a shift at the diner and all the excitement, I plop onto the couch. Looking around at our little house, I think about it filled with baby toys. Of course, we're going to need to clean out the extra room. Right now, it's just a place to toss junk and all of Austin's old sports stuff.

I wish my parents still lived nearby. They would love to have a grandchild. Or I hope that they will. Things haven't been the same since I left college to be with Austin. They didn't think I was ready for such a serious commitment. After the wedding they moved out of state.

"It's our time to enjoy being empty nesters." My mother's voice rings in my head.

After my first big fight with Austin, I called her. What girl wouldn't call her mom for support? She told me it was part of marriage and something I would need to learn to deal with as a mature adult. The relationship I had with my parents was strained after that.

I sit on our old couch, the springs squeaking under me, there are bare spots on the fabric. My eyelids feel heavy as I pull a throw blanket over my shoulders. A short rest won't hurt.

The front door slamming shut startles me awake. Austin stumbles around the living room, mumbling to himself. I glance at the clock on the oven, it's two in the morning.

"Austin? Where have you been?"

"None of your business," he snaps, tossing his keys on the table.

"Babe, it's two in the morning. You got off work hours ago."

He spins around to face me. His blood shot eyes glaring at me like I'm his worst enemy. "Get off my back, Syd."

"I'm not trying to be on your back. I was worried."

"You were asleep on the couch. Real worried," he bites back, stalking to the refrigerator for a beer. "Is there anything to eat?"

"Dinner is in the oven," I say, standing up to fold the blanket. "Would you like me to heat it up?"

"Well, it's not going to heat itself." Austin leans against the counter, downing the can of beer in his hand before grabbing another.

I roll my eyes, taking out the plates of food. One I place in the refrigerator before placing the other in a microwave for him. My appetite is suddenly gone. For a moment I think about taking away the surprise gift I left him, but he sees it before I can do anything.

"What's this?" he asks, picking up the small box. "If it's our anniversary then I forgot."

"It's not our anniversary. But thanks for letting me know you would have forgotten it."

"Don't harp on me, Sydney. What did you waste our money on?"

Before I can snap at him, he tears into the side of the box. He dumps the contents onto the table as if he's looking for the prize in a cereal box. Picking up the pregnancy test and tiny clothing, he goes quiet. But only for a moment.

"What the fuck is this?" Austin's tone is clipped.

"We're having a baby. I'm pregnant."

"Well, I can see that," he snaps, throwing the test on the table. "Who's the father?'

His question is like a knife made of ice, slicing through me in one sharp motion and turning my blood to cold.

"Excuse me?"

"Don't give me that shit. Who have you been fucking around with?'

"Austin, I work all day and then come home to take care of you. The only person I've ever been with is you. How could you ask me that?"

"This is just fucking great. How the fuck are we supposed to raise a baby?"

"Like billions of other people, Austin. We love them and feed them. Provide a safe home for them to grow in."

"With what fucking money, Sydney?"

"We both work, Austin. That's what adults do."

"I got fired!"

His words are out and hang in the air between us. Taking another drink from his beer, Austin's eyes never leave mine.

"Why?"

"Fuck if I know. The manager was a prick. He fired me this afternoon."

"This afternoon? Then where have you been all night?"

"Blowing off steam." Austin finishes the beer and crushes the can before tossing it in the sink. "We're not having a baby."

"What?" My hands immediately go to my stomach. The instinct to protect is already ingrained in my brain.

"There's no way we can afford a baby."

"Then you should have thought about it before coming inside of me all the time."

Austin is across the room with his hands wrapped around my arms. "Don't fucking test me, Sydney."

"You're drunk," I scream in his face. "Let go of me."

"This baby is a mistake."

It's the last thing he says before letting me go and walking out the door. His engine revs in driveway just before I hear the sound squealing tires. When I can't hear the car anymore, I crumble to the floor. My body shakes as I sob, burying my face in my hands.

This isn't how it was supposed to go. We should be celebrating together. All the questions jumble together in my head as I continue to cry.

How could it have gone so badly? How could he lose another job?

"You're not a mistake," I whisper, holding my stomach. "I love you. Mommy loves you."

ten
NOAH

I hated leaving Sydney the way I did. We have things to talk about. I need to tell her not to worry about the car. It's already going to be taken care of without her paying a dime. I've spent years being guarded around people. Purposely not coming back to where I grew up to avoid awkward conversations.

But after seeing her giving so much to help others and watching her care for Tyler alone, she deserves for good things to come to her. If fixing her car is that thing, then so be it. Truth be told, I would give her the world if I thought it would help.

Kissing her only confirmed my feelings for her have not changed since high school. I'm still in love with her.

But right now, my focus is on the phone call I received. My dad was rushed to the hospital with chest pains. Mom called me from the emergency room. Speed limits be damned.

I've barely put the truck in park before I'm out the door. The emergency room lobby is full of people waiting to be seen. I don't see my mom anywhere.

"Excuse me," I say to the woman at the information desk, "my father was brought in by ambulance."

"Patient's last name?" she asks, not even looking up from her computer.

"Reed."

"Room 36, down this hall to the left." She pushes a button on the desk, opening the double doors next to her.

Dad's room is quiet, except the beeping of a machine I assume monitors his heart. His eyes are closed and his breathing is deep. Mom is sitting in a chair beside the bed. Her hand is clasped around his as she watches him sleep. The worry lines on her face, have deepened, making her appear older.

"Hey, Mom," I whisper, coming into the room.

"Hi, honey." Mom stands, wrapping her arms around my waist.

I hug her tightly to my chest and kiss the top of her head. It's almost as if I'm trying to give her all my strength. "How is he?"

"We're waiting for the doctor to come back with the results." She takes her seat again and slips her hand into his. "They gave him something for pain, and he's been resting a bit."

Before I can ask any more questions, there is a knock on the door behind me. A doctor who barely looks old enough to buy beer walks into the room. Am I really getting to the age where everyone looks this young?

Mom gently wakes Dad so they can speak to the doctor. I stand in the corner, ready to call the best cardiologist in the country if needed. One who has grey hair and a pension.

"Hi folks, I'm Dr. Ashcroft from cardiology." He takes a seat on the rolling stool before logging into the computer in the corner. "I have the results of your tests, Mr. Reed."

Mom's grip is so tight around my dad's hand that her knuckles are turning white. I move behind her, putting a reassuring hand on her shoulder.

"It wasn't a heart attack," Dr. Ashcroft tells us. "That's the good news. The bad news is your blood pressure and cholesterol are both high. I'm going to send you home with some medication. But I want you to have a full physical done with your provider as soon as possible."

"I'll schedule it right away," Mom says, finally letting out the breath she was visibly holding. "We're changing how we eat, and we're going to start walking."

"All good points, Mrs. Reed. I'll have a nurse come in with your discharge papers and prescriptions."

Once the doctor leaves, we all let out a collective sigh. I stick around and help until my dad is safely in the car with mom. That poor man probably wishes it had been a heart attack. Mom is about to go into rapid lifestyle change mode and there is nothing he can do about it.

I'll lend a hand by calling my friend, Jack, who happens to be one of the best nutrition and lifestyle coaches in the business. Might as well hook Mom up with the best. Plus, he makes good food, and I know dad will like that. He'll be more likely to stick with it, if he's not forced to eat boiled chicken and steamed broccoli. Just the thought of it makes me shiver.

As for me, today has been a whirlwind of emotions. First the kiss with Sydney and then my dad. It's time for a drink or maybe two. I should at least tell Syd why I left.

ME

> Hey, sorry to dash earlier. My dad was in the emergency room.

POPPY

OMG! Is he ok? Are you ok? Can I do anything?

A smile crosses my lips. That's my poppy always thinking of others. Except she's not mine. I let out a sigh before responding.

ME

He had some chest pains, but they said it wasn't a heart attack. He'll be ok if my mother doesn't annoy him to death.

POPPY

LOL, moms can do that. Or so I hear.

ME

LOL. Listen, I don't want you to worry about your car. I'll take care of it.

POPPY

No way, Noah. I can't let you do that.

ME

I'm not asking. I can handle it.

POPPY

I'm at least paying for parts. Tell me what I owe you.

That's a loaded question. She's never owed me anything. But God, what I would give for her heart. If she said it was mine to have, then I would be the richest man in the world.

ME

We can talk about it. I'll be by in the morning to pick you both up. Good night, poppy. 😊

POPPY

Good night, Noah.

Not far from the auto shop is a sports bar, Lucky's, that's been around since the beginning of time. While it's not a top shelf kind of place, it will do for something to take the edge off.

It's Wednesday night so there isn't a large crowd. Which is just what I'm looking for. I need to talk with Syd about the truth because she deserves that much from me. It's not like she ever did anything to purposely hurt me. She was young and in love. It was just with the wrong guy.

The thought of her with Austin makes me ache. Great, now I'm the one with the chest pains. But unlike my dad, my health is fine. It's the ache of unrequited love since I was fifteen.

I've dated women. When you rub elbows with the wealthy, hot women are a dime a dozen. There was never anything serious. Maybe I was just trying to find companionship to help me make it through a night not thinking about Sydney. I can't believe after all these years my feelings haven't lessened for her.

Feeling her soft lips on mine today was beyond a dream come true. The amount of restraint it took to pull away from her was more than all my dollars in the bank. I can't let myself go further than that. She's a single mother, and I don't live here anymore. It would be easy enough to move back, but is that what she would want? And if she did, what if it didn't work out? I couldn't live here and not be with her. I would have uprooted my life, my company, everything for a woman who already chose someone else once before. I don't want to go through that again. There is also Tyler to consider. He's already had one man abandon him; I wouldn't want to hurt him.

I order a double whiskey from the bartender and take a seat at a table in the corner. Solitude is what I'm used to anyway. It lets me think. A dive bar like this is where I came up with a business model for my first shop.

For what feels like the millionth time I check my emails, waiting for Felicia to tell me who Austin is indebted to. There are different kinds of debt. The kind where debt collectors call your house or dock your pay. Then there is the kind that results in physical harm. Though I honestly wouldn't mind if something happened to him.

Thinking about the idea of Austin James getting his face smashed in is oddly satisfying. Until I hear his voice from the bar.

"Well well well, Noah Reed." His words are slightly slurred and he's leaning as he walks away from the video poker machine.

"Austin." I keep my tone even, trying to avoid what is bound to be a negative interaction.

"I thought you died."

"Nope, just moved away."

"Visiting town and already sniffing around my wife."

Austin stands in front of me with his chest puffed like a peacock.

"Ex-wife," I say, looking him dead in the eye. "I'm just helping her out."

"Helping her out of her pants maybe. She's kind of a sure thing."

I stand so fast that the chair falls over. My blood pumping, fists clenched. Austin has always been a prick. The drunk version is just as annoying. But there is no way I'm going to let him talk about Sydney like that.

"Watch yourself." My voice is low, but my eyes never leave his.

"You are such a fucking sucker for her. I never understood it. Following her like a lost puppy, hoping for a little something." He picks up my drink and shoots it back. "Trust me, it's a forgettable lay."

Before my fist can contact his face, the bartender is between us. She's petite, but clearly not afraid to throw a punch. "No fighting in here."

Austin laughs as he stumbles back to the bar. I watch him before turning my attention to the bartender. "Sorry, I'm not trying to cause a problem." I take a fifty out of my wallet and hand it to her. "For the trouble and whatever dumb thing, he says to you."

"Thanks, doll," she says, tucking the tip in her bra.

Perhaps if it were anyone else, I would feel bad about his fall from the glory of his teenage years. But he made my life hell. He bad mouths Sydney and he ignores his kid. Whatever life hands to him is warranted.

I leave without another look at Austin. He's ordering another drink as the door closes behind me. Let him drink his life away never understanding the things he's ignoring. Austin will always put himself first and that's just pathetic. But he's not worth another moment of my time tonight.

I drive by Sydney's house on my way home. The need to make sure she's ok is so strong I almost knock on the door. But it's late and I don't want to wake up Tyler.

"Good night, poppy."

eleven

SYDNEY

"Lou, I need two specials and a BLT extra crispy bacon."

Today's lunch rush has been the busiest I've seen in a long time. I don't think I have stayed still for longer than it takes to put in an order. My feet are killing me, but the tips are good.

I've barely had time to think about Noah's offer to fix my car. I overslept, and it was a mad dash to get Tyler to school. Tyler excitedly talked about cars with Noah all the way to school. When he dropped me off there was just enough time to say a quick thanks before bolting out of his truck into work.

Although the term overslept implies that sleep was had. I tossed and turned until sometime around three this morning. Austin sent me a late night text that left me emotional. The nerve of him wanting to know if I'm sleeping with Noah.

Austin barely cared about what happened to me when we were married. He hasn't cared at all about me or Tyler since the divorce. But he sees me walking with another man just one time and now I owe him an explanation. Just the thought has me fuming.

"Order up, Syd." Louis yells from behind the counter.

I grab the tray of food, a basket of condiments and make my way to the corner table. When the meals are delivered it's time for me to take a five-minute break. The idea of sitting on an old milk crate in an alley has never sounded so appealing.

Once outside I fish my cell phone out of my apron pocket. There is a text alert from my bank.

Mortgage payment declined. Please contact an account manager.

My stomach plummets to the floor. This has got to be a mistake. With shaking hands, I call the number on my phone.

"Sunrise Community Bank, this is Howard Clifford." The man's voice is pleasant and professional.

"Mr. Clifford, my name is Sydney James. I received a text alert about my mortgage payment being declined." My voice sounds stronger than I feel at this moment.

"I'm happy to look into this for you, may I have your account number?" After I provide the account number, I nervously chew on my lip as I listen to the typing of his keyboard. "Yes Mrs. James it appears the payment was declined for insufficient funds."

"That's not possible. My checking account is with you as well, is there some kind of error in the system."

"I looked into that. But it appears your checking account is overdrawn. Normally we would take funds from your savings account, but there isn't enough to cover."

"I'm sorry, but how is my account overdrawn? I made sure I had enough for the mortgage payment two days ago."

"There appears to have been a large money transfer yesterday. If you think it was fraudulent, I can put a freeze on your accounts. But that doesn't stop the mortgage payment from being overdue. And—"

"Yes, Mr. Howard, I understand. I will get it figured out and come by tomorrow."

"Very well, Mrs. James. See you tomorrow."

My legs won't work. Everything feels numb as I weigh his words. *Overdrawn. Money transfer.* Austin is the only other person with access to that account. We agreed to keep both names on the account for bills and child support. Not that he's ever put a dime into it. But it appears he has no problems taking money out of it.

ME

> Did you transfer money out of my bank account?

AUSTIN

> I told you I needed money. You wouldn't help me, so I helped myself.

ME

> That money was to pay the mortgage! The bank just called. Now there will be late fees. How could you do this?

AUSTIN

> It's not like it was that much. It didn't even cover what I needed. Thanks for nothing.

My eyes sting with angry tears.

ME

> You selfish son of bitch! That money was for the roof over your child's head.

AUSTIN

> I never wanted to have kids.

> I still owe money and need more.

I can't continue this conversation if I have any hope of going back to work. Putting my phone away I do my best to calm my nerves. It's going to take all my tips; the bonus Sal gave me and anything else I can scrape together to pay the bank tomorrow. Sal would give me an advance on my paycheck, but I'm going to need that money for the other bills.

Mustering all my emotional strength I force myself back to work. Maybe this will be the day of that once in a lifetime tip. I shake my head as I walk in the back door.

"Fat chance," I whisper.

The rest of the day continues in a haze of food and customers. I couldn't tell you a single thing that happened after I texted with Austin. I don't even notice when Noah comes in.

"Hey," he says, waving his hands in front of me.

"Hi," I say, attempting to smile.

"What's wrong?"

"What makes you think something is wrong?"

Noah exhales, squaring his shoulders.

"Because I know you. Your smile didn't reach your eyes and I can see where you've been biting your lip."

The wall I put up earlier today is threatening to break, but I don't want to do it at work.

"I can't." My voice comes out as a whisper. "Not here, please."

"Ok, let's get out of here."

I nod, knowing that I'll have to talk about it. Grabbing my purse, I make sure to take the extra food Lou set aside for me. Noah takes the bag from me and presses his hand on my back. His touch is comforting, and I could melt into him right here in the parking lot.

"Why don't you and Tyler come to dinner with me tonight? My treat," he says, opening the truck door for me.

"You don't have to do that."

"Poppy."

His voice sends a shiver down my spine. Noah is standing so close I can feel his words against my neck. Setting the bag on the seat he turns me to face him.

"I want to." Noah cups my cheek with his strong hand. "I want to spend time with you and Tyler. There is so much I need to tell you and I…"

Noah doesn't finish instead he leans in to kiss me again. This time is firmer, his tongue tracing the seam of my lips. When they part his tongue gently caresses mine. His hand moving to the back of my neck while his other pulls my hips closer.

All the tension in shoulders melts away as my body presses against his. His lips are soft, but his kiss his possessive, like he's claiming me. If I'm being honest with myself, being his would be a dream come true.

He pulls away first before whispering, "Have dinner with me."

I'm biting my lip, but this time out of desire. Noah Reed has kissed me twice. If there is a third kiss in our future it might just cause me to combust. This isn't just a reaction from being kissed by a man.

Noah has me aching for more.

twelve

NOAH

"Did you have enough, buddy?"

Tyler nods his head as he grins up at me. Pizza sauce coats his cheek and ice cream drips from his fingers. I'm sure the ice cream was a mistake after dinner, but the kid's eyes were so full of excitement when he saw the sundae on the menu that I couldn't say "no."

"Sticky," he says, wiggling his little digits at me.

"Tyler, don't touch Noah's shirt." Sydney is frantically grabbing napkins. "Baby come here; I need to clean your hands."

Too late, there is a perfect handprint on my shoulder. Tyler and Sydney both freeze, their eyes big as they watch for my reaction. I narrow my eyes at Tyler giving him a big smile. The relief on Syd's face is immediate.

"I think you improved my shirt." I tickle Tyler's side as he squirms in his seat. "It was missing something and now it's perfect."

"See, Mama, I made it better." Tyler says between giggles.

Sydney's smile warms as she wraps her arms around

her little boy. Reaching out she takes my hand in hers, mouthing *thank you*. My fingers intertwine with hers, and I can't help but think that they were made to be there.

It feels so natural to spend the evening with them. There has been laughter and fun. More fun than I've had in years. It's simple, just the three of us eating pizza and ice cream. This night means more to me than any fancy party.

I take her hand in mine again as we walk to my truck. Her soft smile reaches her eyes, which light up, as her cheeks turn pink. When she lightly squeezes my hand back, I know things are never going to be the same between us.

Tyler is softly snoring in his car seat by the time we pull up to the house. The effects of a full belly, sugar crash and the gentle jostling of a car ride. I carry him inside and hold him while Sydney gets his bed ready. We both work to get him changed into pajamas and tucked into bed.

After creeping into the hallway and closing his door the air between us changes. We're alone, just inches apart. Sydney's deep blue eyes search mine seemingly asking me what happens next.

Something snaps and I can't hold back anymore. I push her against the wall, my lips crashing into hers. I grip her hips and push my body against hers. When her lips part, a small moan escapes, before I capture it in my mouth.

Our tongues search for one another, sliding back and forth in a seductive dance. The two times I've kissed her before this have been amazing. But this–this kiss shatters the ceiling on incredible. Sydney's fingers tangle in my hair as she presses against me. The smell of her strawberry shampoo surrounds me. I'm lost in her and never want to be found.

"Noah," she moans, moving her hips against mine.

"Yes?" I pull back to search her eyes. They've darkened with desire.

"What are we doing?" Sydney whispers while smoothing her hands over the front of my shirt. But she doesn't push away. Instead, her fingers twist the fabric, holding our bodies together.

"Nothing that you're not ready for." My voice is a whisper against her cheek. "If this is as far as it goes tonight, that's fine." Tucking hair behind her ear I grab the back of her neck. "But poppy, I've been dreaming of you kissing you like that since high school."

Sydney's cheeks flush as she lets out a shaky breath. "I haven't been –"

"Mama. MAMA!" Tyler's calls get louder.

"I'm right here, baby. I'm coming."

Sydney's eyes look between mine, she looks apologetic, even worried. "I'm sorry. Tyler needs me..."

Part of my heart breaks for her. What has she been through that she thinks she has to apologize for anything?

"No apologies, poppy." I kiss the tip of her nose. "I'll see you tomorrow, beautiful. Lock the door behind me."

Relief visibly washes over her as she nods. Truth is, if she asked me to stay the night, I would without hesitation. But Sydney was in a crap marriage and I'm not about to push her into sex for my own selfish pleasure.

I wait until I hear the deadbolt click before walking to my truck where I immediately adjust myself when I get inside. I'm a guy after all, and I just had my dream girl pinned to a wall. The memory of her soft moan makes me smile as I pull away.

Of course, the memory is quickly tainted with the realization that, once again haven't told her the truth. Why am I hesitating so much? I glance at my reflection in the rearview mirror.

"Hey Syd, while you've been struggling in life, I made millions." My eyes roll as I hear the words come out of my mouth. "You're a fucking idiot."

My phone rings as I continue driving across town. This old truck doesn't have Bluetooth, which I enjoy. Pulling over I take my phone out of my pocket.

"Felicia."

"Boss, I've got your information." There a muffled sound as if she's talking to somebody else in the room. "Sorry about that, I'm... uh... entertaining."

Felicia doesn't simply entertain. If she's not alone it's a safe bet, there is a naked woman in front of her. "If you're busy, this probably could have waited."

"I'm an excellent multi-tasker."

No amount of covering the phone could hide the soft whimper I heard in the background. I give her credit for her dedication to the job.

"Austin James owes money to Steven Richards. Who has a rap sheet for gambling, assault, promoting prostitution and drug trafficking. That's just the stuff he's officially been charged with."

"Fuck." My irritation level has reached chart topping levels.

"Sorry, wish it were better news. If there's nothing else."

"No nothing else. Thank you, Felicia. Happy, eh, dining."

"Naughty," she laughs, ending the call.

I knew Austin was an idiot, but this is on a whole different level of stupid. It's not until I go to toss my phone on the seat that I realize Tyler's car seat is still there. My chest tightens as I think about him. He's such an amazing kid and innocent in all of this. Tossing the truck into drive, I head home. I need to research some criminals.

My eyes feel like sandpaper as I blink against the dim light of my laptop. The last two hours have been spent diving into the deep world of Austin's criminal loan sharks. There isn't much I could find on a simple google search or social media. But Felicia gave me access to some of her investigation sites.

There's no denying that Austin James is fucked. The people he owes money to aren't known for extending their loans. Not without some serious interest or bodily harm. I could care less about his well-being when it comes to his gambling debts. But the asshole's name is still on the mortgage and some other accounts with Sydney.

Scrubbing my hands over my face, it's time to put this away for tonight. I'm going to have to come up with a plan, but my best thinking doesn't happen in front of a computer screen in the middle of the night. I think best when working on an engine. I'll figure this all out while I work on Sydney's car in the morning.

As if she can hear my thoughts my phone lights up with an incoming call from her.

"Thinking about me and can't sleep?" My voice is deep as I think of where a late-night phone call could lead.

"Noah." Her whispered voice instantly sends ice through my veins.

"Syd, what's wrong?"

"Somebody is outside the house. I called the police."

I don't bother with shoes before grabbing my keys and running to my truck.

Speed limits don't matter and neither do a couple of stop signs. Stupid and reckless I know, but there isn't time to concern myself with those things. She's scared and alone while somebody is outside her house. Nothing is going to stop me from getting to her.

"I woke up because I heard a noise outside. Then I saw a shadow move by the window. Noah, I'm scared."

"I'm on my way."

I can hear her shaking through the phone. The ragged inhale and exhale of her breath only make my heart pound faster. She goes quiet for a moment. Before I can ask if she is alright, glass shatters in the background. Sydney's scream pierces my ear like a dagger.

"SYD!" I push the accelerator to the floor. "Sydney, answer me!"

There is a rustling sound on the phone before I hear her voice again. "Noah, they broke the front window. I grabbed Tyler and we're locked in my bathroom."

"I'm coming, baby. Don't talk unless you need to."

Moments pass as I listen to her breathe. Occasionally whispering soothing words to Tyler.

"I hear sirens outside," she whispers, letting out a small cry. "The police are at the door."

"Ok, take Tyler and go to the door. I'll be there soon."

The last few minutes of the drive drag on for an eternity. Every possible scenario is playing in my head. I don't slow until I turn onto her street and see the flashing lights of a police car.

Sydney is standing on the front porch holding Tyler. His little arms wrapped tightly around her neck while she speaks with a police officer. A teddy bear clutched in his hand. When her eyes meet mine, her shoulders relax.

I sprint across the lawn to wrap them both in my arms. Tyler's little arm snakes around my neck as I hold them tightly. Sydney looks up at me and I see the fear in her eyes, as her body trembles against me.

"I'm here," I whisper, kissing the top of her head. "You're safe now, both of you."

thirteen

SYDNEY

I didn't think anything would stop me from shaking. From the moment I heard the noise outside, until Noah showed up, I trembled. When Noah wrapped me in his arms, I felt protected. Not just from tonight's events, but from everything life has been throwing at me.

We stood on the porch, tangled together while the police searched the house. It wasn't until an officer stepped outside holding a large brick that we finally looked around at the damage.

"Ma'am, do you know why somebody would throw this through your window?" The officer holds out the red brick.

"No, sir," I say, glancing at Noah. His jaw is clenched tight.

The officer turns the brick over to show us a message written in thick black marker.

Pay up! Or next time we burn it down.

My stomach instantly contracts. I feel like I'm going to be sick. If Noah didn't have his arm around me, there is no doubt I would have fallen to the ground.

"Austin." I swallow hard trying to keep the rising acid in my stomach from coming out. "My ex-husband, Austin. He told me he needed money to pay somebody back."

"We're going to need his contact information." The officer says, putting the brick into a plastic bag. "Is there someplace you can stay tonight as a precaution?"

Just as I start to shake my head, Noah's arm tightens around me. "They'll be staying with me."

Noah's eyes meet mine making it clear that there is no room for argument. He's not asking me if I would consider it. His mind is made up and, at this moment, I couldn't be more grateful.

One officer follows me inside while I pack some things for myself and Tyler. Noah found some plywood scraps in the garage and is covering the broken window when I return. After giving my contact information to the officers we leave in Noah's truck.

Neither of us talk on the drive. I assumed we would be staying in a hotel room since he doesn't live in town. Instead, we make our way through a neighborhood. Snake along quiet streets, lined with nice cars. Even in the darkness I see larger homes with well-kept yards. A far cry from the tiny homes of my neighborhood.

Noah turns down a long driveway, lined with trees. He pulls the truck to a stop in front large home with a three-car garage. The soft glow of the outdoor lights make the house seem warm and inviting.

"Where are we?" I ask softly so I don't wake Tyler.

"My parent's house. Don't worry they'll be fine with you staying." Noah takes off his seatbelt before taking Tyler out of the truck.

"Noah, I don't want to impose on your parents."

He ignores me as we enter the back door into a large

kitchen. It's the most beautiful place I've ever seen, even in the low dim of undercabinet lights. Just as we close the door the overhead light clicks on, making me jump.

"Hi, honey." A woman's soft voice comes from across the room.

"Hey, Mom," Noah whispers, adjusting Tyler on his arms. "Sorry if we woke you."

"You didn't. Your father is snoring like a grizzly bear." She quickly adjusts her robe when she notices company. "Oh, we have company. Hello, I'm Noah's mother, Sharon."

It's only then that I realize I'm standing in her home in my pajamas. "Nice to meet you, Mrs. Reed." Crossing to her with my hand extended I add, "I'm so sorry for the intr—"

"Mom, this is Sydney and her son, Tyler. They had a break-in at their house, so they'll be staying here."

Noah doesn't let me apologize for coming to his parent's home unannounced in the middle of the night. Mrs. Reed's eyes widen in shock.

"Oh my, you poor thing. Come sit down and call me Sharon, please. Do you need anything? Are you alright?"

I don't have time to answer as Sharon puts her arm around my shoulders guiding me into her kitchen. She's everything you would expect in a mother. I like her immediately.

"I'm fine thank you, Mrs… I mean Sharon."

"Mom, I'm going to put them in the room above the garage, since it connects with mine."

"Of course, honey," Sharon says, patting my hand. "You must be exhausted. Go get settled and please make yourself at home."

I follow Noah up a set of stairs and down a short hallway. He opens the door to a large sitting room. There is a TV on the wall and a u-shaped sectional sofa in the middle. The room is comfortable and warm. For such a large house, the style is not pretentious or stuffy. It's a loving family home.

Noah gently puts Tyler on the couch, pulling out the middle section, converting it into a large bed. Without me having to say a thing, he moves Tyler to the middle and covers him with a blanket.

"There are more blankets in the cabinet under the TV. A full bathroom is through that door and my room is through the other door." Noah points his finger around as he explains the layout.

I nod my head not knowing what to say or do. My emotions are all over the place. I'm torn between wanting to cry, scream or fall into his arms. My hesitation allows him to make the choice for me.

"I'll be right in there if you need anything." Noah says giving me a gentle kiss on the cheek.

The warmth I felt in his arms earlier is gone as soon as he leaves the room.

Sitting alone in the dark I think about all the things happening around me. I decide to let Sal know what happened and that I need a personal day. Then, I email the preschool to let them know Tyler will be out of school as well. I'm not sure when I'll feel safe again.

Grabbing an extra blanket, I lay down next to Tyler. The sound of his tiny snores are like a white noise machine. The rhythmic sound blocks out the storm raging in my mind. Hopefully it will be enough to help me fall asleep.

After twenty minutes of lying there and sleep never coming, I sit up, throwing the blanket off. Maybe I can watch some TV and fall asleep to that. Getting up to look for a remote, the glow of a light is visible under Noah's door. It seems that I'm not the only one not sleeping.

I raise my hand to knock but stop myself. What am I hoping for here? What if he *is* sleeping? What if after tonight he has decided I come with too much baggage?

You're just asking if he knows where the remote control is.

Squaring my shoulders, I softly knock on the door. I don't know why I'm nervous, but my heart is pounding as I wait. After a moment the door opens a crack. Noah is wearing only a pair of sweatpants, his chiseled torso bathed in the soft light of the lamp behind him. I have completely forgotten why I knocked or what my question was.

"Hey, are you ok?" Noah's voice breaks my focus on his delicious looking abs.

"I…um…," I stutter, looking down at my feet. Twisting my fingers together I swallow hard before looking at him again. "Will you hold me?"

Where the hell did that come from?

Noah opens the door wider, stretching his arms out for me to step inside. I press my head against his chest, as his arms cocoon around me. This is better than any blanket I would have found in the cabinet. It's a comfort I didn't realize I was longing for in such a profound way.

His hands feel warm as he lightly strokes my back. Without knowing it we've started to sway slightly back and forth. I'm suddenly slow dancing with Noah, in his room, after somebody broke into my house.

"Why aren't you sleeping?" I whisper, my face still pressed against him.

"Adrenaline probably." The feel of hands slowly drawing circles on my back makes me shiver.

"Your parents have a really beautiful home." I don't know what else to say. "It must have been a nice place to grow up."

"They've only been here a couple of years. But they don't own the house. I—"

"I'm going to lose my house," I blurt out the words with no hesitation. The need to say them out loud greater than I realized.

Noah grows still as he steps back to look at me. "What are you talking about?'

Before I can think better of it, the tears begin to fall, and I tell him everything. "The bank called today. My mortgage payment was declined. Austin took the mortgage money out of the account. He said he needed it to pay his debt. I guess it didn't cover everything since they came to the house tonight.

"I've been trying to pay the bills on my own. Every month I have to decide which ones to pay, but I always make sure the mortgage is there. I have to put a roof over Tyler's head. Austin doesn't care that he took the money from us. How did this happen? How did I let this happen?"

"You didn't *let* anything happen, Sydney. This is all because of Austin's selfishness. Why didn't you tell me?"

"Come on, Noah, what was I supposed to say? We haven't seen each other since high school. I didn't want you to think I was a complete disaster."

"Poppy." Noah nudges my chin up to look at him. "You are the most incredible woman I have ever known. Nothing is going to change that. You are so strong and beautiful."

"I'm falling apart at the seams, and you think I'm strong and beautiful?"

"Since the day I met you," he says, swiping a rogue tear with his thumb. "Can I show you something?"

"Of course."

Noah's eyes hold mine as he takes a step back. Holding his left arm out to his side. Turning his wrist, he shows the inner part of his bicep. In the dim light I see a tattoo. Stepping closer I examine the delicate lines.

A single open poppy.

fourteen

NOAH

I watch as her eyes register the brand on my body. The permanent display of beauty. A mark just for her. It may have been a stupid impulsive teenage decision. But I made sure the artist made it perfect.

"When did you do this?" She asks, running a fingertip over the lines.

Her touch sets my skin on fire. "The day after you told me it was your favorite flower."

"Noah," she gasps, putting her hand over her mouth.

"Is the bad man coming back?" Tyler's voice comes from behind Sydney. We both jump apart as if we were doing something wrong.

"No way, buddy," I say, kneeling in front of him. "You and your mama are safe here with me. I promise he's not coming back."

Tyler squeezes his teddy bear a little tighter to his chest. "Can… can I sleep with you Noah?"

The kid is breaking my heart into a million pieces. I look at Sydney who's standing in stunned silence. Either from my tattoo or Tyler's question. Maybe it's a combination of both.

"Tell you what, let me grab my pillow and we'll have a campout on the couch. All three of us."

"Yay, campout." Tyler excitedly bounces on his toes.

Sydney ushers him into the bathroom for one last potty attempt while I get to work. Grabbing all the pillows and blankets I turn the sofa into a bed fit for a king. Well, a king, his queen and one prince.

Tyler crawls onto the bed snuggling between us. My hand stretched out over my head; I find Sydney's hair. Lightly running my fingers through it until we all fall asleep.

* * *

I wake up first. Tyler has turned himself sideways and his little feet are pushing on my stomach. Moving slowly, I slide out of bed to relieve myself. Tyler is sitting up when I come out.

"Hey buddy, do you need to go to the bathroom?"

He nods his sleepy head, a mop of brown hair flopping into his eyes. Motioning him to come with me, I lead him into my room and show him the bathroom. I toss on a t-shirt while I wait.

"Alright, bathroom business done. Let's find some breakfast while mommy sleeps."

"Ok," Tyler whispers as if we're sharing a secret.

He follows close behind as I walk downstairs to the kitchen. My parents are already awake and sitting in the breakfast nook with coffee.

"Well, good morning." Mom is cheerful as always. But her eyes light up when she spies Tyler hugging my leg. "Hi there, you must be Tyler. My name is Sharon."

"Hi," he whispers, squeezing my leg tighter.

"It's ok, buddy. These are my parents."

It takes ten minutes before he relaxes enough to sit at the table with me. On my lap of course. When he finally accepts a glass of juice from my mom, I know we're on the right track.

"Are you hungry, sweetheart?" Mom asks gently. "I was going to make some pancakes. Would you like to help me?"

Tyler glances at me as if asking for permission.

"He gets pancakes? You fed me egg whites and oatmeal." My dad huffs, folding his newspaper on the table.

"Why did you eat egg whites?" Tyler looks at my dad as if he has two heads.

"Because I'm being punished."

"Were you bad? Mommy says you should always apologize when you're bad." Tyler gets a very serious look as leans towards my dad. "Did you say you were sorry?"

We all share a laugh at the simplicity of his question. Before long, he's standing on a chair next to mom at the kitchen island. She's showing him how to measure and mix all the ingredients for her special silver dollar pancakes.

Knowing he's comfortable I go upstairs to grab my phone. Sydney isn't sleeping when I come in, but the bathroom door is closed. Grabbing my phone off the nightstand I walk to the bathroom. Just as I raise my hand to knock it swings open.

Sydney stands there in nothing but a towel. Her hair piled on top of head. The soft curves of her neck are highlighted by the glow of the bathroom light.

"Hi." Her voice is soft as she lightly bites her lower lip.

"Morning." No other words come out as I take in the sight in front of me.

"I was going to take a shower but forgot the shampoo.

There isn't any in this bathroom." She looks up at me through thick lashes.

"You can use my shower," I say, scanning down her body. Powerless to stop myself from staring too long and wondering what lay beneath that towel. "There's shampoo. I can get you anything else you need."

It takes a moment before remembering I offered my shower but haven't moved a muscle to show her where it is. Silently, I take her hand and lead her into my room to show her my private bathroom.

"Can I get you anything else?"

Sydney turns on the faucet, holding her hand under the water. "Coffee with cream and sugar? If it's not too much trouble."

"No, trouble at all. Be back in a bit."

I've never hustled to the kitchen so fast in my life. Grabbing the requested coffee, I check the progress of the pancakes, then make my way back to the bedroom.

The shower is still running, but the bathroom door is open by a crack. I walk in quietly and set the coffee on the counter, with every intention of leaving. The shower curtain pulls back, and Sydney pops her head out.

"Do you have any conditioner?" She smiles, water droplets running down her exposed shoulder.

Nodding, I open the cabinet under the sink. Finding the conditioner, I hand it to her quickly, to make my exit from the bathroom. My cock is throbbing at seeing a barely dressed Sydney.

I'm pacing back and forth in my bedroom like a caged animal. What am I even waiting for? It's weird that I'm out here listening to her shower. My pulse quickens when the water turns off.

How do I suddenly not know how to act around a woman?

"Noah, are you still out there?"

"Yeah, sorry I'm just leaving."

"Where's Tyler?"

"He's making pancakes with my mom downstairs."

Before I can take a step, the bathroom door opens. Sydney stands in the doorway, naked, wet hair framing her face. Her chest moves up and down seductively as she looks at me.

My cock goes from semi to fully hard in a split second. Every curve of her body is better than anything I've ever pictured.

"Noah," she says, taking a step toward me. "I haven't been with anyone besides my ex-husband. Even then, it's been years."

I take a mental victory lap that she left that asshole's name out of my bedroom.

"This isn't how I pictured it happening when you kissed me the first time." She steps in front of me, her body inches from mine. "But I—"

"Sydney, we don't have to do anything. I would walk out of here right now if you told me to."

"Touch me."

Two words, whispered from her pouty lips undo any will power I had. Grabbing her ass, I lift her off the ground. Those long sexy legs wrap around me, squeezing tight. Our mouths crash together as I move toward my bed.

Pulling back one more time I give her the opportunity to stop this. "We can still stop. If you want to go slow."

Sydney pulls me in for another kiss and sucks my lower lip into her mouth. "We've gone slow enough."

A primal growl comes from deep in my chest as I lay her down on my bed. I can feel the heat of her core through my sweats. Sydney is making quick work of removing my shirt. My hands and mouth exploring every inch of her naked skin.

My tongue circles around one nipple before I sucking it into my mouth. She arches off the bed, letting out a moan. God help me, the sounds each suck is pulling from her, only drives me to do more. I wonder what she would do if I nipped her with my teeth?

"Noah, touch me. Please," she begs, rubbing herself against my crotch.

"You need to come, don't you?" I growl as I take her other nipple in my mouth.

Slowly I slide my fingers down her body towards her bare core, relishing her soft skin. Spreading my fingers I rub on either side, never touching her most sensitive spots.

"Yes, please, Noah." Her breathy pants urge me to do more. "I want you inside me."

"Mmmmm." I hum against her breasts, moving my fingers up and down teasing her more. "What if I want to taste you first?"

Her body stills under me. When I look up, her eyes are wide. "I …"

"When was the last time your pussy was licked, poppy?"

She looks embarrassed, tears forming in her eyes. "When I lost my virginity."

"That selfish bastard." There is a tightening in my jaw as I watch her retract into a shell.

"You don't have to."

"Oh poppy, now more than ever I want to."

Sliding down her body I spread her lips with my fingers. Her perfectly pink core is already glistening. "Look at you so pink and dripping wet for me."

Leaning forward I swipe my tongue along the length of her opening. One long broad lick as I take in her taste.

Her body arches as she moans, her fingers gripping the bed.

With one more long slow lick, I suck her clit into my mouth. Lightly nibbling as it swells in my mouth. Sydney's gasps only spur me into a frenzy. Her taste, her smell, the way her legs spread wider for me. She's perfection.

"You taste so good, poppy. I'm going to make you come on my tongue so I can lick every drop."

My tongue darts in and out of her sweet pussy. Her legs squeeze around my head for a moment until she relaxes into the sensation. I'm relentless with every lick, suck, and nibble. Sydney digs her fingers into my scalp.

"Oh god, yes. Noah right there."

"Is this what you like? What if I add my finger?" I ask, sliding one finger deep inside, curving it to hit her sensitive spot.

"Yes," she hisses, her hips rising off the bed.

Her muscles contract as my finger works in and out. My tongue licks every sweet drop that leaks as she edges closer to climax. Harder and faster, I work her until she's forming a puddle on my bed.

"Come for me." I encourage before flicking my tongue over her again.

Her legs stiffen and her body rocks back before the sweetest release explodes across my tongue. I drink her in, savoring every drop, every moan. When she stills, I remove my finger licking it clean.

Moving up her body I kiss her lips, letting her taste how sweet she really is.

fifteen
SYDNEY

I don't know what just happened or how Noah knew exactly the right way to touch me. To be fair, not even I knew how to touch me. No other sexual experience up to this point even came close to what I just felt.

Sex with Austin always felt more transactional and one-sided. He went down on me once, the first time we had sex. After licking me twice he decided that me sucking his cock would be better. He never put his mouth down there again. I was too embarrassed to ask why.

Noah's strong body stretches over mine as he continues to kiss me and my taste mingling on our tongues. I've never known what it's like to be with somebody who puts me first. Especially in the bedroom. Even now, I can feel how hard he is under his sweats.

Taking a chance with my newfound sexual confidence, I reach between our bodies. Sliding my hand down his chest, over rock hard abs, and under the waistband of his pants. He groans into my mouth as I wrap my fingers around his cock. He is impressively large and so hard.

"Do you want me to suck your dick?" I manage to

whisper, doing some quick mental math to see if he would fit in my mouth.

Noah chuckles softly, "You know how many times I fantasized about you asking me that question?"

"Seriously?" I ponder his question with my hand firmly wrapped around his cock.

"You were kind of my fantasy during high school and college." Noah says bashfully.

"So, you *do* want me to suck you off."

It's not that I'm disappointed to know it. I asked the question after all. But sucking dick has never been my favorite thing. Maybe it was just who's dick was I sucking.

Leaning in, he kisses me again. "I want you to do what YOU want to do to me."

Noah slides his sweatpants down, my hand still lightly stroking him. Swirling the drop of precum under my thumb as I run it down his crown. Both of us stare between our bodies. My bare core just inches from where I'm stroking him.

"I would be happy if you just kept doing that. What do you want, Sydney?"

I lift my hips and brush the tip of him against my soft opening. I'm still wet from the orgasm he gave me. Noah doesn't move, doesn't push himself inside me.

With restraint like I've never seen, he holds himself over me. Allowing me a level of control I've never known. I continue to rub his crown up and down my pussy. Listening as I become wetter with each pass.

It's the ultimate tease for us both, but I'm fascinated with the sensation. The feel of his cock moving up and down. The pressure on my clit and then the slight penetration as he slides between my lips. It's slow and erotic.

"Fuck, baby. This feels so good," Noah whispers in the shell of my ear.

With a firmer stroke, I drag him across me one last time, notching him at my opening. I draw my fingertips along his hips, moving to the firm muscles of his back. Enjoying the feel of his warm skin under my touch as he holds himself above me.

"Noah," I whisper, looking him in the eye. "Please."

With a rumbling growl, Noah sinks into me. I've never felt so full, so complete in my life. He settles his body on mine as we both savor the feeling.

Neither of us talk, just looking at each other, knowing this is a change between us.

Noah begins to slowly rock his hips. I feel every inch of him drag along my inner walls. Wrapping my legs around him, my body moves to meet his. Finding a rhythm so amazing that I'm seeing stars.

"Syd, you feel so fucking good. So tight and wet."

His body moves faster, going deeper with every thrust of his hips.

"Yes, just like that." My nails dig into his back.

Our bodies move on their own, both seeking release. But not for ourselves. No, my body moves to make Noah feel good. His release is the one I'm chasing, and I know he's doing the same for me.

"I'm so close, Syd." Noah pauses for a moment, eyes growing wide. "Shit, protection."

"IUD," I moan not wanting him to stop. "Please don't stop. Come with me."

Noah rocks his hips, again finding his rhythm. The only sound in the room is our bodies moving together. My wetness grows as I climb faster towards the edge. His movements are coming faster and harder.

Just as I fall over the edge with another gushing orgasm, Noah groans his release. Continuing to push deeper as he spills into me. Both of us collapse back to the bed. But he doesn't move from his spot between my legs.

"I could stay buried inside of you. Just like this for the rest of the day."

"I have no objections. But I should probably check on Tyler."

With a mutual groan we reluctantly stand up and return to the bathroom. Noah pulls me into the shower with him and we make quick work of washing each other. He takes his time drying my body with a towel, then helps me get dressed. It's such an intimate time between us. The physical satisfaction of orgasms, leaving our bodies sated. Now the emotional bond we're sharing in the moment is beyond measure.

As we're about to enter the kitchen, Noah stops in the hallway. He has me pressed against the wall in a heartbeat, his lips crashing into mine. He sucks my lower lip between his teeth, as he pulls back.

"I'm not even close to being done with what we just did. I want more of you, poppy."

I'm still blushing as he steps away and struts into the kitchen. Taking a deep breath I follow Noah, doing my best to compose myself after his confession.

"Mommy, I made pancakes." Tyler exclaims, bouncing in his seat.

"Good morning, Sydney. Are you hungry?" Sharon asks as she sets down a plate piled with pancakes.

"Starving," I say, looking meaningfully at Noah.

His eyes still have heat in them as he leans against the counter sipping a cup of coffee.

"Sydney, this is my dad." Noah motions toward the man sitting next to Sharon. "Dad, this is Sydney."

The man's eyes are soft as he gives me a warm smile.

Standing he extends his hand, "Mike Reed, it's nice to meet you."

Introductions complete, Noah pulls a chair out for me before taking the one to my right. The morning is spent enjoying pancakes, coffee, juice, and warm conversation.

It's the most relaxed I have felt in years. Noah's parents are genuine and kind. Austin's parents only ever regarded me as his wife. An accessory to be seen and not heard on most occasions.

Noah's hand rests firmly on my leg under the table. It's a possessive gesture that somehow feels right. Like he's telling me that I'm safe.

After breakfast, I insist on helping with dishes. Mike takes Tyler into the living room to watch cartoons.

"What do you two have planned today?" Sharon asks, cheerfully drying dishes with a towel.

"I should check on things for the opening this weekend."

When their attention turns to me, the happy bubble of the morning bursts. The reality of my life comes crashing down on my shoulders.

"I took a personal day from work and told Tyler's school he wouldn't be in. I should probably check in with the police. But I also need to go to the bank." In all the chaos of last night I didn't grab the money I stashed in my dresser. "Noah, I need to go by the house too. I'm sorry to ask if you can drive me today."

"It's not a problem, anything you need."

"Tyler can stay here with us." Sharon adds as if it's the most natural thing in the world.

"I can't ask you to do that."

"Nonsense. You didn't ask. I'm insisting. He can't run errands with you all day. He can help me in the garden and I'm sure Mike has some tinkering in the garage to do."

My heart swells with this woman's words. His own blood relatives wouldn't offer to watch Tyler.

"Thank you, Sharon."

"Oh, sweetheart," Sharon says, wrapping me in a hug.

A motherly hug feels foreign to me. The last time my mother hugged me was after Tyler was born. But it was cold, distant, and felt like she was doing it out of obligation. Nothing like Sharon, who holds me tight, softly humming as she does.

One thing is for sure the Reed family is exactly the family I wanted for Tyler. It hurts that I haven't been able to provide that for him.

"We should get going," Noah says, pulling me out of my own mental spiral.

He's good at that.

sixteen

NOAH

SYDNEY HAS BEEN QUIET SINCE WE LEFT MY PARENT'S house. I'm trying to give her whatever support she needs.

After feeling her body against mine this morning, I'm lost in my own head. The moment I was inside her, I felt it. She's mine. There's no way I can go back to a life without her, again. My hand hasn't moved from her thigh since we got in my truck.

Her house looks different this morning. With the plywood on the window, the chipped paint stands out more. The tall weeds in the yard are glaring at me. She's been doing her best to continue making this a home for Tyler. But the little house looks run down, tired, and sad.

I hold her hand as we walk up the front steps. She's shaking as we reach the front door

"Let me check the house before you go inside," I say, taking the key from her.

She only nods as she looks at the plywood.

"This was supposed to be Tyler's safe place. Maybe I should just let the bank take it."

Her words gut me. Not because she's talking about

giving up this crappy house. But because she's talking about giving up. Sydney looks tired and worn down like her home.

"Wait here for a second." I open the door and make quick work of checking each room. "Ok, it's alright to come in."

There is no light in her eyes as she walks inside. Without a word she walks to the back bedroom and pulls an envelope out of a dresser draw. She looks at the contents closely the clutches it to her chest.

"Thank you." She whispers to herself.

I know she's not thanking me, but thanking God or the universe that her money is still there. She doesn't have to show me what's inside for me to know. I'm willing to bet it's every bit of money she has left right now.

"Why don't you pack a few more things? You and Tyler can stay with us a little longer."

"You can't keep coming to my rescue."

"Says who?" Wrapping my arms around her, I hold tight. "I'm here for you. Whatever you need."

"You must have a life you're missing out on."

"Grab whatever you and Tyler need for the rest of the week. Then we're going to take a little drive. I want to talk to you about something."

Sydney packs while I check some emails and send a message to Felicia.

ME

> His debt collectors threatened his ex-wife and son. They are staying with me. I need you to have a few things rush delivered to my parent's house.

FELICIA

Yes, sir. Anything else?

SAFE WITH ME

> ME
> Clear my schedule for the next week. I'm staying in town a little longer.

FELICIA

Should I ask?

> ME
> I pay you not to.

FELICIA

You pay me to keep other people from asking.

> ME
> Emailing you a list of what I need. Same day delivery.

FELICIA

Yes, boss. 😊

I roll my eyes at her last message. That "yes, boss" is her way of telling me she'll find out what she wants to know. It doesn't bother me, and I'll tell her, but not this morning. Right now, I need to tell Sydney the truth about my business.

Sydney comes out a few minutes later with two bags. I take them from her as we walk to my truck. Her eyes are locked on her feet the whole time. The envelope still clutched in her hand.

"Can we stop at the bank first?" Her voice is hoarse and barely above a whisper. "I need to make this payment."

"Of course. Tell me where to go."

She directs me to her bank but asks me to wait in the truck as she goes inside. Her embarrassment is written all over her. Almost like a giant scarlet letter. My anger towards Austin grows with each step she takes towards the bank.

I should call the bank and pay off her loan. It would be so easy for me to do. But I think it would upset her more. She's such a proud woman, even when she's stubborn. I know Sydney would give the shirt off her back to anyone in need. Yet, she refuses to ask for help. Even in a circumstance that was created by somebody else.

When she returns to the truck I see it on her face. It didn't go well.

"Do you want to talk about it?"

"They accepted the payment after some pleading. They are also going to take Austin off my checking and savings accounts. There are late fees that I'll owe for the mortgage. Because the mortgage and his credit card were opened with both of us, we have to share those. So, his debt is mine as well because it happened while we were married."

Sydney sucks back the tears I know are forming. "I would like to help." I offer gently.

"You've done more than enough. Was there something you wanted to talk about?"

I hate talking about money under good circumstances. But she needs to know. Nodding, I start the truck and drive to the new auto shop. Thomas won't be there today, so we'll have it to ourselves.

"What are we doing here?" She asks, looking out the window.

"Come on, I'll explain inside."

I unlock the front door and usher her inside. After punching in the alarm code and making sure the door is locked, I walk her into the garage.

"Noah, I don't want you to get in trouble with your boss. I probably shouldn't be in here."

"We're going to work on your car." I tell her, pulling her along behind me. "Don't worry about the boss."

"Noah, don't jeopardize your job for me." Sydney stops, pulling her hand from mine.

Pinching the bridge of my nose I let out a breath. I had a plan in my head on how I was going to do this. Once we started working on her engine and she was helping me work, then I would tell her. While her stubbornness is usually a turn-on, right now, it's throwing a monkey wrench in my plans.

"I am the boss, Syd." I watch for any kind of negative response. "I'm the owner."

"Why didn't you tell me? You've always loved cars. I think it's great you're opening your own shop."

Sydney stands on her tiptoes, placing a kiss on my cheek.

"Syd," I say, cupping her cheek in my hand. "I own all of them."

"All of what?"

"This shop is the fourteenth that I've opened. I own the entire company." I pull out my wallet and take out my business card, waiting as she reads it over.

Noah Reed, CEO
Jensen Automotive

"The company? You have your own company?"

Sydney steps away from me, her hand going to her forehead. Her eyes are darting back and forth as she processes what I've just told her. Her fingers brushing over the print on the tiny card naming me as CEO.

Laughter rolls out of her. There's no telling if it's happy, sad, or some kind of emotional break. She's just laughing.

"I don't even own a car," she gasps, holding her stomach. "But you own …" She motions for me to keep talking.

"The company. My parent's house, an apartment in the city, a private plane, and vacation property."

Her eyes are wide as she nods her head.

"I've been wanting to tell you. I just wasn't sure how to bring it up."

"Sure, sure. I can see how that might feel weird. I'm broke and crashing on your parent's couch. Which you own."

"At first, it was more about protecting myself. Nobody here knows about my wealth. I usually go to a town for an opening and then go back to the city. People are always vying to be friends with the rich guy for the perks."

"You thought I would use you?" She searches my eyes for the truth.

"Sorry." I tell her, reaching for her shoulder.

"I get it. I'm a broke single mother who showed up in your life with a mountain of debt and a deadbeat ex."

"Syd, I keep my life a secret from everyone but my parents. We haven't seen each other in a long time, and things are very different. Although the more time we spend together the more I realize you are still the caring person you've always been. You aren't being nice because I have money."

"I'm not." She steps closer, wrapping her arms around me. "I'm just happy you're here with me."

"Me too, poppy." I tighten my arms around her. "Now come on, I'm going to teach you about cars."

We spent the rest of the afternoon working on her car. Sydney helps me gather parts and tools and doesn't mind getting dirty as she turns wrenches along with me. There are still some things to work on, but we make a good amount of progress on her car.

"How much is this all going to cost Noah?"

I shake my head at her, as I wipe a dirt spot off her

cheek. She's beautiful, even with motor oil and dirt on her face.

"Don't worry about it. I know the owner." I give her a wink as I wipe grease from my hands.

"I'm at least paying for parts. Since I'm doing the labor."

That's the Sydney I remember feisty, stubborn, and determined.

seventeen

SYDNEY

After the shock of Noah's confession, I wasn't sure how to feel. Until he made me work on a dirty engine with him. He may have money, but he works hard. There is no doubt that he's earned every dime in his bank account. However big it may be.

He's finishing the last of today's repairs while I clean up. The new shop is so clean, I feel bad making any kind of mess. At one point he asked me to grab a part and I brought every option I found in the supply closet.

Standing on a rolling staircase I restock everything we didn't use. My skin warms and a blush spread across my cheeks when I feel Noah's eyes on me.

"Enjoying the view," I ask, wiggling my butt from side to side.

"Best view I've ever had."

Noah holds the stairs as I climb down into his arms. He holds me tight, kissing me as deeply as I wrap my legs around his strong frame.

I want to please him. I want Noah to understand that I'm with *him*, not the rich business owners that he is.

Rocking my hips forward, I moan at the sensation of him growing hard under me. I've never felt such a sense of sensuality. It's a powerful feeling.

"Noah?" Even with this newfound confidence, I'm a little shy to ask. "I want to try things…with you."

Hesitantly I pull back, searching for reassurance. "What kind of things, poppy?"

"Things I've never tried or have never been able to enjoy. In bed, I mean."

"Look at me." Noah sets me down, cradling my cheek. His eyes are dark and full of desire. "We can try anything you want, with one rule."

"Ok." My stomach is in knots. What if I can't handle his rule?

"If you don't like something, don't feel comfortable. Then we stop and cross it off the list. What we do together has to be about pleasing both of us. Understand?"

I could cry at this moment, but I don't want to ruin the mood. Noah just gave me a sexual freedom like I've never known. "Will you tell me if I could do something better?"

A chuckle vibrates through his chest. "I promise to be honest with you. Is there something you're worried about?"

"Blowjobs," I whisper the words, my eyes shifting down.

"Hmmmm, well first let's get rid of that phrase."

My head cocks to the side, my eyebrows scrunching together. "What do you mean?"

Noah steps back, closing the supply room door. When he turns around, I feel like prey being hunted. His eyes locked on mine as he steps toward me.

"This isn't high school. We're not sneaking behind the bleachers in the gym. Although, that would have been fun." Noah stops in front of me, the outline of his hard cock clear in his work pants. "Tell me you want to suck my cock."

"Can I suck your cock?" Again, my voice is just a whisper.

"Poppy." His tone is firmer, coming from somewhere deep in his chest. "I don't want you to ask. I want you to tell me that you WANT to suck my cock."

Power, this is about power. Noah doesn't want me to be a meek mouse in the bedroom. He's giving me the choice to make it happen. Closing my eyes, I summon all my confidence, before glancing at him.

"I want to suck your cock, Noah."

"Good girl," he says, undoing his belt, then lowering the zipper of his pants. "On your knees, poppy."

Moving to the floor, I sit back on my knees just in front of him. I slowly run my hands up his legs, to his waistband. My eyes never leave his. "Tell me if it's not ok."

Noah only nods, his eyes still burning into mine. Grabbing the waist of his pants, I drag them down slowly, along with his briefs. Delighting in the sight of his generous cock springing out in front of me. I'm still not sure how much of him I can fit in my mouth.

Wrapping my hand around his base, I give him a gentle squeeze, sliding my hand up to the tip. A low growl from Noah is the only sound in the small space. I follow the same path with my tongue. Licking the underside from base to tip, before swirling my tongue around his crown. Tasting the salty drop of precum I've coaxed out.

Licking my lips, I take a breath and wrap my lips around him. Pushing him inside my mouth as far as I can take.

"Fuck." Noah hisses out, sucking air between his teeth.

I freeze, his cock still in my mouth, looking up at him.

"Don't stop now, poppy." Noah winks before pulling my hair away from my face. He holds it in his grasp, firm enough to feel controlling, but still allowing me to move.

Using my hand and mouth I move his cock in and out of my mouth. My tongue dragging the underside, as my hand follows behind it. I start slow, allowing myself time to adjust to his girth. As my confidence grows, I take him deeper. Hollowing my cheeks to suck as my head bobs.

I've never enjoyed doing this as much as I do right now. Noah's deep rumbling moans excite me. Knowing I'm bringing him pleasure like this has my pussy wet and throbbing.

"So good." He moans, letting his head fall back.

I smile around his cock, before taking him as deep as I can. Feeling his tip reach the back of my throat.

Noah's moan is the loudest I've heard from him. When I look up his eyes are wide, his mouth open as he pants. Keeping our eyes locked, I do it again and again. His hips rocking forward slightly.

"Poppy, fuck, my good girl. I'm going to come. Do you want to take it in your mouth?"

I don't think twice before pumping his cock harder and faster. A new desperation takes over me. I never allowed Austin to come in my mouth. Noah would be the first man to ever do it. I want to give this to him. I want him to have something that I've never shared.

"Sydney, I'm close. If you don't want—"

"Come in my mouth, Noah." I say quickly, sucking him between my lips once again.

Caressing him with my mouth, using everything I can to bring his release. His grip on my hair tightens and his hips move faster. My free hand moves up his leg to grasp his balls. I roll them in my hand, giving a firm squeeze as I continue sucking his cock. One last trip to the back of my mouth and he growls his release.

Jets of hot come fill my throat. I pull him back slightly to swallow it all. His taste, his sounds, all of it turns me on.

My pussy drips as I swallow every drop. Still on my knees I watch as his eyes flutter open with a look of satisfaction on his face.

"How was that?"

Noah tucks himself away, adjusting his pants before pulling me to my feet. "I can barely see straight. You are so fucking perfect."

A smile slowly forms on my lips, as he pulls me close.

"I want to bend you over that work bench. But we should get going. I'm sure mom is making dinner already. Raincheck?"

Nodding my head, I kiss him one more time. "I hope Tyler wasn't too much trouble today."

"Not a chance. She's always wanted grandkids."

Noah's lips snap shut after the words are out. Neither of us say a word at first. His eyes wide, as I stare back at him.

"Why haven't you?" I whisper, still holding myself close to him.

My eyes search his with the question. Waiting for him to crush my spirits by telling me he loves being a rich bachelor who never wants to be tied down.

"You were taken."

People say that the greatest three words a man can say are 'I love you.' I will argue that until the day I die. Austin told me he loved me, and it was just words. The words you're obligated to tell the person you marry. He never loved me the way I should have been loved.

But in this moment, the words, *'you were taken,'* mean more than anything else.

"Let's go see what's for dinner." I suggest, sneaking another kiss.

I make Noah move the car seat to the floor, so I can sit next to him in the truck. My head resting on his shoulder as we carve our way through town.

Commercial buildings, turning into small row homes and tiny yards. After a while the homes and yards grow bigger until we're pulling into the driveway of the Reed home.

Tyler comes running out to us the moment we are parked. He's dirty from head to toe, but his smile is bigger than I've ever seen.

"Mama! Noah!"

"Hey, Bud," Noah says, bending down to scoop Tyler in his arms. "You look like you've been busy."

Tyler proudly looks at this dirty shirt. "Yup, I helped in the garden and then I fixed the lawn mower."

"You did? Well, that sounds like an honest day's work." Noah smiles at him.

"He's been a big help today." Mike says as he walks out of the garage. "I'm not sure I would have got that stubborn lawn mower going if it weren't for Tyler."

My little boy beams with pride. I do what I can for him, but a boy needs a father in his life. He needs days of getting dirty and playing with tools.

"Dinner's ready!" Sharon calls from the back door.

"Tyler, don't touch anything. Go straight to the bathroom and wash your hands." Guiding him by the shoulders towards the nearest bathroom, I watch to make sure he doesn't get dirt on anything.

"Awe man, that's the worst."

Noah laughs before I turn to him with an eyebrow raised. "You too, mister. Go wash your hands."

"Awe man," he quips, smacking my ass as he walks by.

Sharon is happily puttering around the kitchen as things bubble away on the stove.

"Can I help with anything?" I ask, washing my hands.

"Everything is almost done. Would you mind setting the table?"

"Not at all." I grab the plates and cups she's already set on the counter.

With the table set and the boys' hands washed, we sit down to a feast. Sharon made roasted chicken with mashed potatoes and fresh sauteed carrots. Tyler even eats them, telling me they are way better than frozen.

Everyone helps clean up then it's time to take Tyler upstairs for a much-needed bath. To my surprise, Noah had bags for things delivered for us today. Bubble bath, body wash, a few small cars for Tyler and even my favorite strawberry shampoo.

"Did you have a good day?"

"Uh huh, it was the best." Tyler plays with the bubbles in the tub. Making a giant bubble mountain. "Can we stay here?"

"We will for a little while. Don't you want to go home?"

"No, I like it here."

"I do too." I scrub his little face with a cloth, "but we will have to go home eventually, ok?"

I see the look of disappointment in his eyes, I feel the same way. Being here has felt so different from what we are used to. The house is big, fancy and new, although it's more than that. The Reed's are kind, loving, and have treated us as if we are part of their family.

After his bath, Tyler falls asleep halfway through the book I packed for him. A day of playing outside and a full belly does wonders for a kid. Watching him peacefully hold his little teddy bear, I make a promise for the both of us. "We'll be ok. I'm going to make sure it gets better."

"He knows." Noah's hushed voice comes from his bedroom door behind me.

"Knows what?" I ask, turning to face him.

"That you'll make it better."

"That makes one of us." I tell him letting out a frustrated sigh.

"Do you want to watch a movie? We can watch in my room, so it doesn't wake him."

"What do you have in mind?"

"Oh, definitely porn."

I'm holding back the laughter, so I don't wake Tyler. Getting up I follow Noah into his room, shaking my head.

"What? I'll let you pick which one."

"Terrible," I say, climbing on his bed. "For that we're watching a rom com."

"Fine, but I get to see your boobs after."

He narrowly dodges the pillow I toss at him. Laughter comes so easily around him. There isn't this feeling of dread like at any moment things are going to erupt. Being around him is easy, even now that I know about all his success.

He's still just Noah, the sweet guy I met in high school. Who hasn't made a move while I'm sitting next to him watching a movie. After what we did on his bed this morning, I figured 'watch a movie' was just code for sex. But aside from holding my hand, he's been a perfect gentleman.

"I can't believe you made me watch that." Noah sighs, turning off the movie.

"Notting Hill is a great movie." I tell him, stretching my arms over my head. "Besides, it's a good starter rom com. We haven't even gotten to my favorite yet."

"What's your favorite?"

"Nope, not telling. You'll just have to stick around and find out."

Noah wraps his arm around my waist pulling me on top of him. My legs straddling his lap while his hand snakes to the back of my neck. Holding my gaze, his eyes search mine. He swallows hard, "you want me to stick around?"

"I like being around you. It's always been easy, comfortable." I lower my eyes, unable to look at him for the next part. "But I know you'll have to leave."

"I have options, poppy," he whispers, stroking my cheek. "We don't have to figure it all out right this minute. But there are options for us."

"Us?" I risk a glance at him.

Noah's eyes are bright, and he has a devilish smile. "Yeah, us."

Leaning forward I kiss him. Not intending to start anything, just to thank him for being so wonderful. But the moment his lip's part for mine, the fire ignites inside me.

"Can I tell you a secret?" I ask him, moving my hips against him.

"Always." His hands grip my ass, grinding me along his cock. Small moans escape our lips, lingering in the charged air between us.

"I've never swallowed before," I say, kissing his neck. "You were my first."

Noah's hand stills my hips. After a moment he takes a deep breath. He moves off the bed, checking on Tyler before closing the bedroom door. The rest of night is spent in a tangle of sheets, sighs, and pleasure like I've never experienced.

Neither of us stopping until the early hours of the morning, when exhaustion finally overcomes us both.

Noah pulls my body against his. My back firmly pressed against his front and his head buried in the crook of my neck.

Sleep takes me quickly now that I am nestled in his arms. My safe place.

eighteen
SYDNEY

This weekend has been like something out of a Hallmark movie or one of those sappy romance books I've always loved. Noah and his family have welcomed Tyler and I into their home with such open, and loving, arms. Speaking of loving arms, waking up in Noah's is a dream come true. I don't think he let's me go all night, because I fall asleep being held and wake up with him still wrapped around me.

He drove Tyler to school this morning so I could get a little extra rest on my day off. The king size bed in his room is the most comfortable thing I've ever slept on. The idea of lying in bed all day is very tempting. However, there is the very real task of talking to my insurance company about the break in and trying to get my window fixed.

With a reluctant sigh I roll out of bed to get ready for the day. I'll need to ask about doing laundry since I didn't pack very many things to wear. Although I suppose running short on underwear is a sign that it's time to return to my house. The reality of that idea sits like a rock in my stomach as I walk towards the kitchen.

"How does she expect me to eat this? Where are is the good stuff?" Mike is grumbling to himself, while digging through the contents of the pantry.

While I've been feeling like this is a fairytale, Mike feels like he's being punished. Until he's able to meet with his doctor Sharon has put him on a very strict diet. She even tossed his favorite snacks into garbage as he watched in horror.

"Good morning," I say, eyeing him cautiously from the doorway.

Mike straightens his back as if he's been caught doing something, or eating something he shouldn't. His head turns towards me slowly, his cheeks round and full. His eyes are wide and there is a rosy pink to his cheeks. "Busted," he mumbles around a mouth full of food.

Crossing my arms over my chest, I raise a questioning eyebrow. "What's for breakfast, Mike?"

He swallows hard before pleading with me. "Don't tell Sharon."

Laughing softly to myself I walk around the counter to stand in front of him. "Come on big guy, let me see," I say, holding out my hand.

Mike sheepishly puts an empty bag of mini blueberry muffins in my hand. "She's got me eating roughage and cardboard. How's a man supposed to live like that?"

I sympathize with him, even though I know Sharon's heart is in the right place. She wants her husband to be healthy and live a long life with her. The two of them together is what relationship goals are made of.

It isn't hard to see the loving glances they give each other, or the way Mike always kisses her forehead before leaving the house. Even if he's just going to the garage.

"Come on, I'll make us some egg whites and turkey bacon." I pat him on the shoulder before tossing the wrapper in the trash.

"That is not breakfast, it's a slow form of torture. You should save yourself and have some real food."

Ignoring his continued protest, I set to work gathering ingredients around the kitchen. Mike pour's himself a cup of coffee before sitting at the kitchen island while I work on breakfast. I can feel him grimace with every new vegetable I start to chop.

"Why don't you tell me what it is you don't like about these foods?" I ask, ripping a kale leaf into small pieces.

"I must sound like a giant man-child about all of this." He rubs the back of his neck, while blowing out a big breath. "Maybe it's more about the sudden change. Eggs, potatoes, and bacon are what I'm used to. Plus, bacon is, well bacon."

I don't respond to him, but motion for him to keep talking as I chop broccoli, tomatoes, and mushrooms.

"I've worked hard my whole life, sometimes barely scrapping buy when Noah was a kid. Breakfast and Dinner were the hearty meals. Sharon wanted us to start and end the day with full bellies. Noah always had school lunches, but there were days that we didn't have much for me to take to work."

My heart aches with understanding. "I can understand that. There have been plenty of times I wasn't sure we would have enough to eat. Lucky for us I work in a restaurant."

"Sydney, I didn't mean to -"

"No, please don't apologize. I just know exactly what you mean about certain food feeling important, comforting or even special." I crack an egg and separate the white from the yolk, repeating the process several times. "Perhaps we can look at this current situation another way. Look at all the vegetables that Sharon grew, think how amazing it is that your wife did this with her two hands and some love."

Mike's eyes roam over the variety of vegetables on the counter. A soft smile creasing the lines around his eyes, his chest swelling with pride. "She is wonderful at it. We didn't have enough space for her to have a garden when Noah was little."

"Now you do, and she's turned the tables on you. It's her putting the food on the table while you enjoy so well-deserved relaxation after years of working so hard. Breakfast should be ready in about ten minutes. Why don't you go get Sharon?"

Mike happily saunters out of the kitchen to find the love of his life. I sauté the vegetables in a pan, with some fresh herbs, also from the garden. While they soften, I put the kale in a blender with some fresh strawberries, a banana, some mangos from the freezer and a little almond milk.

Sharon and Mike join me in the kitchen just as I'm pulling the turkey bacon out of the oven.

"What's all this?" Sharon smiles as she looks at the feast laid out on the counter.

"Sweetheart," Mike says, taking her hand. "I have been fighting you on this new way of eating, but I understand now just how blessed I am. The love of my life grew most of this food for me and I took how lucky we are for granted."

Sharon's eyes glisten as she smiles up at her husband. "I love you, even when you're stubborn."

"Have a seat," I say, holding up two plates of food. "Breakfast is served. Our special today is vegetable scramble, turkey bacon and a fruit smoothie."

Mike pulls out a chair for Sharon before taking his seat.

I wait anxiously as he tries the food. Even with his new appreciation for vegetables I see the reluctance in his eyes. He raises a forkful of scrambled egg whites to his face, sniffing it first, before trying it. I'm biting the inside of my cheek as I watch his jaw move. He doesn't say anything as he takes a drink of his smoothie. Finally, Mike picks up a piece of turkey bacon, wrinkling his nose as he moves it to his lips. He doesn't know that I spiced it up a little bit. Sharon and I glance at each other, neither of us speaking while we wait.

"Well Sydney, I gave it a try." Mike wipes his mouth with napkin before continuing, my gut twisting as I wait. "Darlin, this is delicious. How did you make turkey bacon taste good?"

Sharon and I jump out of our seats with excited screams. She wraps her arms around me for a tight hug. "Thank you, sweetheart."

"What's going on in here?" Noah's voice breaks through our excited laughter.

"Sydney, made breakfast and your father likes my vegetables." Sharon says, with her arms still firmly wrapped around me.

My eyes meet Noah's as he tilts his head in question. Sharon releases me from her gracious hug, and I make my way to the extra food on the stove. "Sit down and I'll make you a plate."

I set a plate in front of Noah, waiting nervously as he takes a bite. He eats far heathier than his father, this meal isn't a stretch for him.

"This is delicious, dad's right you made turkey bacon taste good."

My cheeks warm from the praise being showered on me.

"Sydney, teach me your secret," Sharon pleads, giving my hand a gentle squeeze.

"Well mixed maple syrup, garlic powder and a little bit of cayenne pepper to brush over the bacon before I baked it in the oven." I giggle as Mike happily munches on another piece, washing it down with the last of his smoothie. "And I put kale in the fruit smoothie."

The room falls quiet as Mike pauses mid-sip, his eyes wide. He slowly puts the glass down as if I had just told him it was laced with poison. "You hid vegetables in my smoothie?"

Pressing my lips together I try to hold in a laugh. "I do the same thing with Tyler's smoothies."

Laughter erupts around the table.

"I've got my eye on you, sneaky Syd," Mike laughs, pointing his fingers at his eyes then at me.

The Reed family is so supportive and loving, I feel like I belong with them. But that also comes with the realization that this is temporary. Still my feelings for them are growing stronger, especially for Noah.

As I sit there lost in my own whirlwind of thoughts, he places his hand on my thigh. His fingertips floating across my skin, sending a tingle of excitement up my spine.

"Come on, let's go for a drive," he says, gripping my thigh, a seductive twinkle in eyes.

"I need to do the dishes first."

"No ma'am." Mike's voice is firm as he collects the empty breakfast plates. "You cooked, so we'll clean up."

"Mike's right, Sydney. You kids go enjoy the day." Sharon puts her arm around Mike, "besides getting this one to eat vegetables earns you a free pass on dish duty."

Noah takes my hand and leads me to his truck. When he opens the door for me to get inside, there is corsage laying on the seat. A beautiful mix of roses, baby's breath, and poppies. I open my mouth to speak, but only a small gasp falls from my lips.

"I thought we could go on a real date today, jus the two of us." Noah reaches in picking up the wristlet of flowers, "you don't have to wear it, I just wanted -"

Grabbing Noah's face between my hands I pull his lips to mine. There are no words that could express how I feel. I put every emotion into kissing him, praying that he would be able to feel what I can't verbalize.

Slowly, I pull my lips from his, not saying anything as we stand wrapped in each other's arms. When his gaze meets mine, I can feel it, deep in my soul.

I'm in love with Noah.

nineteen

NOAH

It's finally happening, I'm taking Sydney on a date. I realize it's a silly thing to be excited about since we have firmly planted ourselves in the *more than just friends* category. This is different though, it's something I have wanted to do for almost fifteen years.

The corsage was a definite must for today. If my dream of a date with Sydney was coming true, then her dream of a poppy corsage was too.

She sits on the bench seat next to me, her fingers drawing slow circles on the back of my neck. Her touch sets me on fire. The hand I have resting on her thigh, draws the same slow circles across her skin. The shorts she has on, show off her gorgeous legs.

You need to focus, Noah.

We make our way out of town, heading towards the coastline. It's takes about an hour for us to reach the spot I picked for our date. The drive goes quickly as we laugh and talk, she even convinces me to sin along with the radio.

Sydney raises a questioning eyebrow when I pull off

the highway into a wooded area. "Should I be worried that you drove me out to the middle of nowhere?"

I smile leaning in for a kiss, "maybe I want to know how loud you can scream my name."

Sydney moans into my mouth my tongue brushes hers. I tangle my hands into her hair holding her in place deepening our kiss. Just as she reaches for the front of my jeans I pull back. "Come on, poppy. I have a date planned for us and if you touch me, we'll never leave the truck."

I wouldn't mind spending the day with her riding my lap in the front seat. Maybe after I show her what I planned. Grabbing the backpack, I hid in the truck bed, I lead her towards a small trail.

It's peaceful as we walk along the winding path, into the thick trees. Sydney doesn't ask where we're going or complain about the fact that she's wearing sandals on a hike. The forest thickens, just before opening to a small, secluded beach. The dirt trial disappearing under our feet as it changes to sand.

"Wow, this is amazing." Sydney takes in a deep breath as coastal breeze blows off the water. She wastes no time taking off her sandals to wiggle her toes in the warm sand.

We walk until we find a place to sit halfway between the tree line and crashing waves. As she takes in the view of the blue water, I set down the backpack to empty its contents.

I spread a blanket on the sand, before laying out the picnic I prepared. It would have easy to splurge on champagne and fancy cheeses, she's worth it. But I kept it simple with sandwiches, fruit, and some bottled waters.

"What's all this?" Sydney asks, kneeling on the blanket next to me.

"I thought we could have a picnic on the beach." I pop a grape in my mouth as she survey's the food, her face unreadable. "Unless you want to go somewhere to eat. There's a good bistro up the road a little."

"Noah, this is perfect. I almost expected you to pull out a bag of -"

With a triumphant smile I pull a bag of barbeque potato chips from the backpack, along with a bottle of Coke to share. "I wouldn't forget the important stuff."

Sydney snuggles into my side as we take our time enjoying the food and the view.

"Penny for your thoughts," Sydney says, laying her head on my shoulder.

"I was just thinking about how long I've waited to take you on a date. I'm sorry it took so long."

Sydney looks at the flowers on her arm, "why didn't you ask me out in high school?"

Her question takes me by surprise, it certainly wasn't because I didn't want to. "I didn't think I was good enough. You were popular and hung out with the jocks. I was just a nobody who hung out in auto shop."

Sydney gently squeezes my arm, "you were always good enough. I'm sorry if I ever made you feel like you weren't."

"Do you remember the day you told me about wanting that corsage? You asked if I was going to prom, and I told you it wasn't for me." Sydney nods her head. "I was planning to ask you."

"What?" She sits up straight turning to face me.

"I had been saving up my money so that I could take you to a fancy dinner and rent a limo." My eyes search hers as her hand covers her mouth. "The day Austin asked you, was the day I planned to ask you. He beat me to it, and I saw how excited you were when he did."

"I wanted you to ask me." Her voice is soft, as a rogue tear slides down her cheek. "The dream I had about prom night, where I told you that I saw everything. It was you. I kept waiting, and hinting. I thought you only saw me as a friend."

My heart cracks with her confession. She could have been mine. I let the notion that I didn't belong in her world win over the dream of being with her. Guilt creeps in as I realize that if she had gone with me, she might not have married Austin.

"I should have ..." I swallow the lump in my throat, unable to stop the *what if 's* that are swirling in my mind.

"Hey," she says, placing her hand on my cheek. "What did we know as teenagers? So we both held in our real feelings."

"If I had asked you, then you may not have married that asshole. Your life could have been different."

"That's true. But Noah, if it had gone a different way, I wouldn't have Tyler. Would you have left town to pursue the career you have? We can't play the game of what could have been. We're here now." Her eyes drop the blanket as she adds, "even if you'll be leaving soon."

The reality of our current situation hits me head on. It feels like my heart is beating in the rhythm of a ticking clock. A clock that is counting down until she goes back to her house, and I leave town. "You could come with me."

"Noah, we can't make a rush decision in the heat of the moment. I have Tyler to think about, plus my job and the house. Which reminds me I need to call the insurance company today."

"I know you're right." I let out a sigh, before cupping her cheek. "Stay with me the rest of the week. I don't want to waste any of the time we have."

"I can't impose on your parents like that. Plus, Tyler and I don't have enough clothes for the week."

"We can stop at your place to pick up more things. Or

I'll buy you new clothes. My parents will be thrilled to have you and Tyler there. I think they love you as much as I do."

The words roll of my lips so easily it hardly registers that I've said them. Sydney's eyes grow wide as we look at each other. After everything we just confessed to each other I'm not going to waste another minute.

I pull her into my arms, her legs straddling my lap. "I'm not going to take that back. We've wasted too many years, but you don't have to say it back right now. Just please tell me you'll stay with me, and we can discuss our future."

Sydney wraps her arms around my neck before nodding her head yes. I pull her in for a kiss, my hands grab her hips, pulling her against me. "We should head back soon," she says, against my lips. "I'll need time to pack more clothes."

We take our time gathering up the remnants of our picnic, then begin our drive back to town. Neither of us has said much since she agreed to stay with me. But there is an energy in the air between us. My grip on her thigh is dangerous high, as she runs her finger up and down my arm.

The closer we get to town the more my fingers draw up and down her skin. I move my hand between her legs, rubbing along the outside of her shorts. Sydney widens her legs, granting me access. She moans as she nuzzles into the crook of my neck

"How's your focus, Noah?"

"Getting harder by the second, along with my cock."

She lets out a breathy giggle as she runs her tongue along my jaw. "Let's see how well you can multi-task."

Sydney unbuckles her seat belt, shimming her shorts off, and lays down on the bench seat. She has one leg on the floor and other propped on the seat. The only thing separating her pussy from my eyes is a thin piece of fabric, which is already soaking wet.

"Keep your eyes on the road," she says, moving my hand up her thigh. "Make me come while you drive."

Her hand moves the thin fabric of her panties out of the way. This is going to be the hottest thing I've ever done, and the most dangerous. I run my fingertips along her seem, feeling her soft folds are already dripping wet.

I grip the steering wheel harder trying to focus on the road, as I slide two fingers into Sydney. She lets out a satisfied moan, as her warmth wraps around my fingers. I move them in and out of her slowly, allowing my rhythm to match the gentle curves of the road. With each stroke of my fingers, Sydney grows wetter, her breathing growing heavier with each pleasure filled sigh.

Her fingertips grazing across my hand, forces my eyes to look down at her. The vision of her laying on my truck seat, with her legs spread for me, will forever be burned into my memory. She parts her pouty lips as she cries out when I curve my fingers inside her. I glance at the road, before returning my sights to Sydney as she plays with her clit.

"That's right, poppy. Play with that beautiful pussy."

The road straightens out, allowing me to increase the speed of my fingers which are drenched with her wetness. Sydney pants and moans as my name rolls off her lips.

Our fingers work together as she arches against the seat, her cries growing louder. "Scream for me, Syd."

"Fuck yes, Noah. Don't stop. I'm so close."

My fingers move faster as I rub her sensitive bundle of nerves. She matches my speed, with her fingers moving across her clit.

"I'm coming. Oh God, NOAH!"

Her pussy squeezes my fingers, as wave of cum spills

from her, soaking the seat. I slow my strokes against her inner walls as she comes down from her climax. When her hips collapse against the seat, I pull them out, sucking them clean. Enjoying the sweet taste of her orgasm as it drips down my hand.

I return my focus to the road, while Sydney shimmies her shorts into place. She sits up to lean over placing a kiss on my cheek.

"It's your turn. Keep those eyes on the road and both hands on the wheel," she whispers, while she unzips my jeans.

"Fuck, Syd." My voice is a rasped hiss as her fingers wrap around my cock.

Sydney smiles as her head moves to my lap. I have to focus on not pushing the accelerator to the floor when she takes me in her mouth. It's growing difficult to keep my eyes on the road, as her head bobs up and down on my cock. When she sucks me to the back of her throat, I let out a primal growl.

This feeling is too good not to enjoy without distraction. There is a forest service road just a head and without hesitation I jerk the wheel to turn off the highway. Driving far enough down the road that my truck isn't visible before putting shifting into park.

I wrap my hands in Sydney's hair, pulling it back so I can watch as she takes my cock in her mouth. "I want to hear you Noah," she says, before taking me to the back of her throat.

"Fuck poppy, keep going. I love seeing my cock in your mouth."

I let my head fall back against the seat, as she sucks harder, swallowing when I touch the back of her throat. I don't hold back any moans of pleasure with every lick and suck, until the tightening in my groan becomes too much.

Gripping her hair tighter, my hips buck as I roar my release, filling her throat with spurts of cum.

"FUCK POPPY"

This woman just gave me the single best experience I've ever had in a vehicle.

twenty
NOAH

Nothing in the world could compare to the sight of Sydney with her legs spread open in my truck. The road head that followed is a close second. After I came in her mouth, I could barely stand. It's a miracle we made it home.

Even now, days and many rounds of sex later, I still can't shake the perfection of the image in my head.

When she confessed I'm the first to come in her mouth a dam broke inside me. I spent the rest of that night and into the early morning hours devouring her. I made her come on my face, my hands and cock.

A greedy smile still crosses my face as I think about it. I adjust myself before checking my tie one more time in the mirror.

The new auto shop opens this morning, and Tyler's birthday party at the park is set this afternoon. I've arranged for a petting zoo, bounce house, and magic show.

Because Sydney hadn't invited anyone to a party she couldn't afford, I reached out to Sal, who handled getting the word out about his birthday bash. It's going to be a perfect day.

"You clean up nice." Sydney's voice comes from behind me.

My heart races knowing she's here.

"What are you doing here? I thought you had to work."

"I am. Just took a little break to run over here and wish you luck."

My stomach drops knowing by "run over," she may have literally run here. Her car isn't finished, but I moved it out of the shop for the opening. Not that it matters. I have a surprise for her.

Her smile changes when I turn around. "What is it? Is there something on my suit?"

"No," she says, looking me up and down. "I've never seen you in suit. It's really sexy."

The corners of my curl into a smile. "Sexy?"

Sydney steps into the office, closing the door. "Very. If I thought there was time, I would show you how sexy, right here."

I snake my arms round her waist, grabbing her full ass. "I can make time," I whisper, bringing my lips to hers.

"Mmmm, I wish. I need to get back to the diner." She nibbles my lower lip before pulling away. "But maybe you can wear this for me again."

Reluctantly, I let her pull away. I've never wanted to wear a suit to bed so much in my life. Fuck, I'll wear one every day if it gets her this excited.

"Before you go," I say, adjusting my now rock-hard cock. "I have something for you. Close your eyes."

With a skeptical look, Sydney closes her eyes. Taking her hands in mine, I carefully led her outside. She looks beautiful tilting her chin upward as the sunlight warms her face. Moving her into just the right spot, I stand behind her. Inhaling her strawberry scent, enjoying one selfish moment.

"Open your eyes," I whisper in her ear resting my hands on her hips.

It takes a moment for her eyes to adjust to the bright sunlight. Sydney lets out a small gasp as everything comes into focus. Sitting in front of her is a new crossover SUV. Nothing big, but just enough room for Tyler to grow. It's safe, reliable, and most important paid for.

"Noah, what is this?" She turns to look at me as I hold the keys up.

"Your car won't be ready before I have to leave. You and Tyler need something you can count on."

"But I can't afford a new car." Her eyes fill with tears, and I see the fear. There is also the sadness at the mention of leaving.

"You don't have to afford anything." I put the key in her hand. "It's yours."

"I can't take this. It's too much." Sydney tries to shove the key back.

"Sydney, you're going to be late. You can argue with me about this later."

"Oh no, we're going to do this now."

"Ok, consider it a loaner car then. Something to use until your car is done."

I know she wants to argue with me, but she'll lose. She also knows it's time for her to go back to work, and she's too loyal of an employee to shrug off returning.

"This conversation is not over," she says, glaring at me.

Leaning in, I kiss her deeply and pull her body close to mine. "We can fight about it in my bedroom tonight. I'll see you in the park this afternoon."

I don't give her the option to argue, opening the car

door and ushering her inside. She's biting her lip as she looks at the new interior. Yes, I splurged on all the upgrades because she and Tyler are worth it.

There is a small moment of satisfaction as she starts the car and closes the door. But I see the eye roll as she drives away. I do enjoy her sass.

If she only knew the amount of money I would spend on her. I hope to show her one day. There needs to be more time between us, though. It would be stupid to drop to my knee after such a short time. She would run for the hills or worse reject me on the spot.

Satisfied that I partially won this round I make my way inside again. I have a business to open. These things aren't done with a lot of pomp and circumstance. It's not a big hotel or museum, but there is a small gathering of employees, their families, some local vendors, and a reporter from the local newspaper.

After answering a few softball questions about the business, I hand everything over to Thomas. He looks nervous as hell in his button-down shirt and slacks. His young wife beams next to him, her belly only slightly showing.

"It's a big day, Thomas," I say, offering my hand. "Congratulations."

"Thank you, sir. I hope to make you proud."

"It's not about me, Thomas. Make your family proud." I glance at his wife's hand as she places it on her stomach. "Do you know what you're having?"

"A little girl."

"Well let me be the first to give her a gift." I hand the keys to Sydney's car to Thomas. "It still needs work, which you'll have to do. But the shop is yours in the off hours and all the parts can be expensed to the shop."

"Sir, I can't—"

"You're right," I chuckle, taking the key from him to hand to his wife. "But she can."

"You'll need a second car once the baby comes. It's not new and Thomas will have to do a lot of work. But I think it should be ready in time."

I'm almost knocked over by Thomas' wife as wraps me in a hug. Do I treat all my employees like this? No. But I'm a sucker for being young and in love. These two are off to a good start and they both work hard. They should be rewarded for it.

With the new shop open and customers already calling for appointments, I turn it over to Thomas.

I have someplace to be.

I'm giddy with the idea of a kids' birthday party. The thought of having kids isn't foreign to me. I just put it to the side in favor of work. Most of the women who have passed through my life weren't interested in settling down. They wanted to jet-set. I'm not a man whore, there haven't been many women. But none I would ever consider settling down with.

Sydney on the other hand, was my perfect girl in high school. She's still perfect to me. Every minute around her and Tyler makes me long for more. Just because it would be stupid to ask her to marry me already, doesn't mean I can't tell her how I feel.

Yeah, I'm giddy with the idea of this party.

twenty-one
SYDNEY

"Tyler, sweetheart, slow down. The playground isn't going anywhere," I call out as he runs full speed towards the swings.

It was Noah's idea to spend the afternoon in the park. With everything happening lately, I didn't have it in me to plan a party. Let alone the funds. But an afternoon in the park is free and always fun.

"How did the opening go?" I ask Noah, as we walk after Tyler, his fingers laced with mine.

I'm still planning to argue with him about the car, but at least I can ask about his morning.

"It went well. This garage has potential to be my most successful one yet."

"Because of the location?"

"That and I put somebody in charge who has the drive to make it happen."

Noah slows and pulls me to a stop. "Speaking of Thomas. I gave his wife your car."

"I'm sorry, you what?"

"They are expecting a baby. I gave them your car so Thomas can fix it up before the delivery date."

My ears are ringing, and I feel a sudden headache coming on. "You gave away my car."

"Yes," he says, placing his hands in his pockets. "But I replaced it with a new one."

"Noah, it wasn't yours to give away, and we still need to discuss the other car."

My frustration is reaching a new level when I hear Tyler screaming. All focus on arguing with Noah is gone as I scan the playground. Nobody else looks panicked, which only fuels my nervousness.

How could no other parents be looking to find a shrieking child?

It doesn't take long before I find him. He's not hurt or afraid, he's shouting with excitement. Just behind the playground a large birthday party is set up for Tyler.

There is a large banner wishing him a happy birthday. Every child from his preschool is running around. Sal and Lou are passing out party hats. Sharon and Mike are standing guard over the cake.

Everything my little boy wanted is in one spot. Balloons, streamers, friends, food, a bounce house, magician, and even a petting zoo. Something he most definitely did not ask for but is there just the same.

"Mommy! Mommy! All of my friends are here, can I go play?" Tyler screams, running toward me at full speed.

"Of course," I choke out, at a loss for words. "Enjoy, sweetheart."

I turn my attention to Noah. He's looking at his feet and trying to hide a sheepish smile, as he rocks back and forth on his heels. "I may have done more than just the car."

"I'm furious, happy, sad, and excited all at the same time. We will talk about this later."

My "mom voice" must have worked because Noah's smile fades. "Can we enjoy the cake first? A dead man walking needs his last meal."

I hate he's making me laugh and love him for it.

That thought is new. Do I love Noah? Yes, he's been amazing while since we've been together. Today, however, he's made me feel awkward and weird. I'm not even sure if those are the right words for it.

Unfortunately, I have no time to think about it. There are twenty preschool-aged children running wild, with two goats and a donkey nearby. We haven't even gotten to the cake yet. Though, it dawns on me that Austin may not know about the party.

Grabbing my phone, I decide it's better to invite him than have him hear about it later. I may not care about him anymore, but he's Tyler's father.

ME

> Hey, we're having a last-minute party at the park for Tyler's birthday. If you're available, you should stop by.

AUSTIN

Cool

ME

> Does that mean you'll be here?

AUSTIN

Don't know, busy. If I'm there I'm there.

ME

> It's your son's fifth birthday. You could at least come see him.

AUSTIN

Stop being a bitch. I'll try to stop by.

Letting out a frustrated sigh, I tuck my phone into the pocket of my jeans. I shouldn't have said anything to him, but I'm trying to be the bigger person. Austin could easily decide he wants to fight me for custody one day. Playing nice now, only works in my favor.

The festivities go into the late afternoon, before we start to see the telltale signs of burnout in the kids. A massive sugar crash and over stimulation has taken its toll. I thank the parents as they cart their over-tired kids to their cars.

Tyler is asleep on Sal's lap as I pack up the last of the cake. For all the mixed emotions I had about today, Noah really did make my little boy feel special, which is more than I can say for his father who never showed up.

To my relief, Tyler didn't ask about whether his father would be there. Even after dinner and his bath, he happily hugged Noah and me before falling asleep.

Noah is working at the desk in his room when I get out of the shower. He seems to understand I need some alone time and doesn't try to intrude, which only leaves me feeling more conflicted.

"Do you still want to discuss everything?" His voice is soft, but he doesn't turn away from his computer.

"I don't want to fight." I fidget with the hem of the t-shirt I'm wearing. Noah's t-shirt that I stole from his closet.

"I didn't say fight," he says, turning around. "But if I did, then you wouldn't be fighting fair dressed like that."

I let out a half laugh, one that doesn't make it to my eyes. Noah moves to sit at the edge of the bed and motions for me to join him.

"Is this sad look still about the car and party?"

"No, well not completely. Can we put a pin in that conversation for right now?"

"Sure." Noah slides a little closer to me, wrapping an arm around my waist. "So, tell me what's going on?"

"I texted Austin today, to tell him about the birthday party."

The tension in Noah's jaw is instantly visible. He inhales slowly before letting out a long breath.

"And?"

"And nothing. That's just it. He didn't bother showing up to his own son's birthday party. He told me 'Not to be a bitch about it'."

"Fucking bastard," Noah says under his breath. "Why do you even try?"

"I just want Tyler to have a father in his life. Plus, I worry one day he'll change his mind and try to fight for custody. If I play nice now maybe he won't try it."

I pick at an imaginary string along the hem of the shirt. "My parents didn't call; his parents didn't call. All these people are blood relatives and didn't bother to acknowledge my little boy."

"I'm sorry, Sydney."

"Thank you for making him feel special."

"He is." Noah tilts my chin up, "and so are you."

"Noah, what are we doing? You'll be leaving soon."

"That doesn't have to mean anything."

"But it will." I move away from his touch, instantly missing his heat. "I can handle it if you leave and don't come back. I mean it's going to hurt, but I know I'll be okay. But Tyler, he's already been abandoned by everyone who should love him."

"Sydney, what are you saying?" He's off the bed and reaching for me.

"Maybe we should take a step back. Figure things out

between you and me first. If that has to be a long distance relationship, then sure. But it's for the best if you take us back to our house tomorrow."

"We don't know if it's safe for you to be there."

"I'll figure it out. The longer Tyler is here the more he gets used to it."

"So, let him get used to it."

I don't want to fight with Noah, not after everything he's done for us. Yet I can't help the surge of emotions that overtake me. He needs to understand where I'm coming from and why this is important.

"No." My voice is strong even if I feel like I am crumbling. "No, I'm not going to let him get used to it. Because eventually you'll go back to wherever you live, and we'll go back home. To our shitty rundown house I can't afford. I can't let him get heartbroken again and again when things get taken away from him."

"What do you think I'm going to do? Do you think I'm going to leave and never come back?"

"I don't know, Noah. But you keep tossing money around in front of him like it's nothing."

"It *is* nothing. It's just money."

"It's nothing when you have it. It's everything when you don't," I spit the words at him with all the anger I have left. "You buy a car I didn't ask for and give away the one I worked for. Without talking to me. You put on this elaborate birthday for my son without talking to me. I'm not a kept woman. I should get to have a say in things."

"I should be allowed to spend my money."

"Spend *your* money, Noah. Do whatever you want. But don't think you can buy my submission or affection. I've already had one man treat me like a voiceless doll. I'm not going to let it happen again."

Noah steps back as if I slapped him in the face. I see

anger in his eyes, but it's also outlined with hurt. I don't give him a chance to respond before I walk out of his bedroom and close the door behind me.

I pack the few things and leave before dawn, giving a thank you note for Sharon and Mike.

Everything aches when I carry Tyler into our tiny house. He shivers as I lay him in his bed. I grab an extra blanket to cover him before wiping a tear from my cheek.

I promised to make things better, but somehow, I think I just made it all worse.

twenty-two
NOAH

Noah,
I don't know what happens next. I'm sorry.
Sydney

I'VE READ HER NOTE A DOZEN TIMES ALREADY THIS morning. I tossed on some jeans and sweatshirt with every intention of going after her. There isn't a rational thought in my head, though. Anything I want to do could only push her away more. She would hate me throwing money at this, but maybe I can do something to help her situation another way.

"Noah Wesley Reed." Mom stands in the doorway of my room after yelling my full name. Suddenly I'm twelve years old bringing home a snake from the park. "Why is there a two-page thank you letter from Sydney on my counter?"

"I'll fix- two pages? I got one line." I grab the letter from her hand, scanning its contents.

"Excuse me, this is my letter," she says, grabbing the paper. "Seems to me you have some fixing to do."

"I'm going to, I promise. But I need to leave for a couple days."

My mind is moving a million miles per hour. Mom just stands in silence as I race around the room grabbing everything I need.

"You're going to leave without telling her?"

Her question pauses my frantic thoughts. "You told me to fix things. I'm going to fix things."

Staring at me over the rim of her glasses, she squints her eyes as if she's not sure what she's watching unfold.

"Don't let her get away."

Without another word she walks out of my room. I grab my phone and text Felicia.

ME

> Returning today. Have the plane ready by 3PM. Also, get me a video conference with my attorney within the hour.

FELICIA

> You realize it's Sunday morning and I was in the middle of hot yoga.

ME

> Is that her name? Yoga?

FELICIA

> Do you really want me to answer that?

ME

> No. Make the arrangements.
>
> Please.

FELICIA

Good boy! The plane is already fueled. I'll have your pilot there and ready by 2:45PM. Your attorney will be live on video conference in 30.

ME

One more favor. I'm going to need an address.

I change into my suit while I wait for the video conference. Once I have the documents I want him to draft, I need to make two stops before going to the airport. Today is all about business and I'm damn good at that.

* * *

His apartment is exactly what I pictured it would be. Worn down, dirty, and well past its prime. Not unlike Austin. The curtains on the front window are open enough for me to see him passed out on the couch.

I hammer my fist against the door until he wakes up, stumbling to the door.

"What do you want?" He squints his bloodshot eyes against the midday sunlight.

"I have a proposition for you," I tell him flatly.

"Sydney send you to collect child support? 'Cause I don't have shit to pay her."

"I'm here on my own with a business deal." I prevent him from closing the door in my face by placing my foot between the door and its frame. "I know how much money you owe and what they'll do to collect it. It would be to your benefit to hear me out."

Austin looks me up and down, like he's sizing up an opponent. It's comical really. Once upon a time I would have backed down. Today I'm looking down at him. The disheveled shell of somebody I once feared. Now I barely pity him. My deal is for Sydney and Tyler, not him.

He walks back to the couch leaving me at the open door. *Motherfucker.*

Stepping inside I close out the fresh air and sunlight. The apartment is dark, dirty, and smells like stale beer. There is a new TV mounted to the bare wall, the only nice thing in the place. Interesting purchase for a guy who claims to be broke.

"I don't have anything but beer and tap water."

"This won't take long," I say, stepping closer to the sofa.

Beer cans litter the coffee table. A child's drawing underneath them. The words *To Daddy* along the top. Sydney mentioned Tyler was learning to write his letters. She no doubt smiled as she told him how to spell out the words. The thought of her smiling as they color together fills me with a strange blend of warmth and rage.

This pile of shit has no regard for either of them. His son's drawing is being used as a damn coaster. The skin on my hands feels tight as I flex my fingers. It would take nothing for me to call his bookie and have him dealt with. It's still an option, but I came here with an offer.

I am a businessman after all.

"Good, because the game is coming on soon."

I roll the tension out of my neck before getting right to the point.

"I'll square your debts and even buy a one-way ticket to wherever you want to go."

Austin snickers like the giant man child he is. He's playing like I offended him, but I see the gleam in his eyes. He has never had to face consequences in life. Now I'm giving him a way out of his debts.

"You must love this. Swooping in to bail out the

popular guy." He raises his chin like a proud peacock. "The outcast nobody cared about helping the star quarterback."

"We've been out of school for over ten years."

"You're still jealous," Austin sneers, narrowing his eyes at me.

"Jealous?" I let a small smirk dance across my lips.

"You hated me in school for being everything you couldn't be." Austin stands as he ticks things off on his fingers. "Popular, athletic, wanted by all the girls."

I stay firmly planted where I am. Austin will never be able to live as anything more than what he was in his self-proclaimed glory days.

"Not all the girls."

"Oh, that's right," he says, smiling at me with a crooked grin. "You always had a crush on Sydney."

Her name on his lips makes my jaw clench. The bastard is on shaky ground, but I'll let him keep digging his own grave.

"Yeah, it must eat at you that I finally got her. God, she was a hot piece of ass." Austin licks his lips as he talks about her. "Then she had a kid and let herself go. Tits sagging and that pussy was never the same."

It takes less than a second for my hand to clamp around his throat. His back is against the thin living room wall before he can blink.

"Watch your mouth," I warn through clenched teeth. My face inches from his. "I would think very carefully about your next words. My offer can go away, and the debt collectors will come calling. I'll make sure of it."

Austin's face reddens as he stares back at me. "You think this will get her attention? That she'll suddenly feel something for you?"

"No." My fingers squeeze a little harder, watching his

face redden. "Neither of us is worthy of her. I'm at least man enough to not screw with her life."

Releasing him, I back away and let him slouch against the wall. He sucks in air as I remove an envelope from my coat, tossing it on the coffee table.

Austin picks it up, eyeing me as he turns it over in his hand. "What's the catch? You're not doing this out of the kindness of your heart." He pulls out the stack of paperwork I had drafted by my attorney.

"You're going to sign these today," I say, handing him a pen.

"What is it?" He glances over the documents, but I'm sure he's just looking for a dollar amount.

"The first removes you from the mortgage on Sydney's house. It puts everything in her name." I wait a moment before going on. I want to see the look in his eyes for this part. "The second signs over your parental rights to Tyler."

Austin's face hardens, but I know it's a smoke show. He looks over the paperwork, reading each line while twisting the pen between his fingers.

"How much will you give me?"

"I already told you. Your debts will be gone and a plane ticket to a location of your choosing."

"What makes you think I want to sign over rights to my kid?"

I straighten my coat and tug at the cuff to my sleeve before looking at him. Narrowing my eyes at the man who could have been something once. "Because if you gave two shits about him then you would have punched me the second I told you what that paper was for."

Austin scribbles his name across the paperwork before shoving it back at me. "I want to go to Vegas."

"Be at the airport by ten tonight," I tell him, tucking the paperwork into my coat. "There will be a ticket under your name." Without another word I walk to the front door.

"Hey, what about the money I owe?"

My grip on the doorknob tightens. "I paid your bookie off this morning."

I knew he would sign the paperwork with the promise of money. Austin going to Las Vegas gets him out of Sydney and Tyler's lives which is all I care about. The money I paid is worth it, but a lost cause for Austin. He's going to Las Vegas where nobody is going to bail him out.

I give him less than a year before he's homeless or dead. My lips curl into a grin at the thought of the latter.

twenty-three
SYDNEY

I HAVE NEVER BEEN SO TIRED IN MY LIFE EVEN WHEN TYLER had colic as a baby. Noah and I haven't talked since I left his parent's house almost two weeks ago. I keep reminding myself it's for the best. Which I almost believe during the day. But at night, when I'm lying in bed alone, everything hurts.

The memories of his touch replay over and over again when I close my eyes but then I wake up to a cold house and an empty bed. It's the same as it was before he came back into my life. I'm alone and raising a child. Everything is the exact same without Noah here, but somehow it feels harder.

Sal didn't ask questions when I told her I wanted as many overtime shifts as possible. I work every morning after dropping Tyler off at school. The afternoon is spent with him until I go back to work the dinner shift. The first night was hard, because I had to take him with me.

The second day Sharon showed up at the diner to check on us. When I told her Tyler was in the back, she all but ran to hug him. She insisted on watching him while I worked. I agreed with the condition she and Mike watch him at our house.

They won't allow me to pay them anything. It warms my heart to see Tyler with them. His own blood relatives ignore him, but Sharon and Mike treat him like he's a Reed. Mike even fixed a few things around the house.

We haven't discussed Noah, which I'm grateful for. Although I wonder if it's their choice or his request. I didn't think we would stop talking altogether, but I suppose it's what I get for leaving him with a one-line note.

"Order up, Syd." Lou is working the breakfast shift with me today.

"Thanks, Lou," I smile, lifting the plates of eggs and bacon.

"You look tired."

"Oh good, I was afraid my makeup would cover the bags under my eyes."

Lou tilts his head, smiling softly. "I meant you're working too hard, Sydney. You need to take some time for you."

It's sweet when Lou shows his softer side.

"Thank you. But I've got bills to pay and an ex-husband who seems to have disappeared."

"I'll marry you. You can make an honest man out of me." Lou wipes his brow with the dish towel on his shoulder. "Come on, Syd. What do you say?"

"She says no, you crazy weirdo," Sal yells from behind him. "Sydney can do a hell of a lot better."

Lou clutches his heart as if wounded. These two are crazy about each other, even if they don't show it in front of people. I only know because I caught them kissing in the walk-in freezer once. I've never said anything, and they would never tell me the truth anyway.

"Sydney, I need to speak with you for a moment." Sally motions me to follow her as she walks to her office.

Once again, I feel like a kid in trouble at school. Walking into her office, Sal has paperwork spread out on her desk. I swallow hard before closing the door.

"Sydney, I can't keep giving you the overtime waitress shifts."

I'm sitting down, yet it feels like the world is spinning around me. Maybe I can get a second job, something part time with a similar schedule.

"I understand. Thank you for letting me work as much as possible."

"I'm making some staffing changes, and I'll need your apron as well."

The rug just went out from underneath me. "Am I being fired?"

"As a waitress, yes." Sal doesn't look at me as she shuffles some papers. "As my new manager, no. You'll start that on Monday morning."

It takes a moment for me to register what she's saying. "Your new what?"

"Sydney, you've been working here for years. You don't miss work, stay late, take on extra shifts, and you started a community soup kitchen. I want you to run things for me here so I can take a step back. This is purely a selfish promotion on my part."

"You're promoting me? To manager?" There's suddenly not enough air in her office. The edge of my vision blurs with tears.

Sal turns on her small desk fan and points it at me. "Calm down, Sydney. You're going to pass out if you don't take a breath."

"Sally, this is-I can't-it's just—" Frustrated with my

brain not forming words, I blow out a breath. "Thank you."

"You've earned it and more, Syd. So go home. Enjoy your weekend. Monday morning you start managing this place."

I can't hold back my appreciation as I wrap my arms around her. "Thank you, Sal. Thank you so much."

"We love you here, honey. We love Tyler, too."

Lou gives me the nod of approval as I hang my apron on a hook in the kitchen. "See you Monday, boss lady."

It's too early to pick Tyler up from school. After wearing a waitress uniform for years, I decided to raid my closet for work clothes. Not that it's anything fancy but getting a choice in what I wear is going to be a nice change.

My happy bubble bursts when I pull a letter from the bank out of the mailbox. Throwing my head back, I let out a sigh before opening the white envelope of doom.

"Well, Syd, what is it this time? Overdue payment? Increased interest rate? You didn't pay for lunch one time sophomore year of high school, and they want to collect that, too?"

I scan the letter once, looking for words like *overdue* or *foreclosure*

This surely has to be a mistake, I think immediately after reading the document.

Rolling my eyes, I shove the letter into my purse. Looking at clothes will have to wait because now I have to talk to somebody at the bank. Just when I thought today was looking up.

The line isn't very long, and it doesn't take long for me to talk to somebody. Unfortunately, they tell me I'll have to talk to a mortgage specialist and send me to sit in the lobby and wait.

Twenty anxious minutes later my name, a slender woman with chestnut-colored hair calls my name and I make my way to her desk.

"Good afternoon, I'm Sheila. I understand you have some questions about your mortgage." She motions for me to take a seat.

"Yes, ma'am. I received this letter, and I'm a little confused by it."

"Ok, I'm happy to help with that. May I see the letter, please?"

Handing the envelope across her desk, I wait as my foot bounces on the floor.

"I see there was a change on your account. We send these letters as written confirmation of the change for your records."

"But I didn't make any changes. Is there a way to find out who did?"

Sheila types into her computer, bringing up my account before scanning her screen. "It says here that Austin James signed over all rights to the mortgage and removed you from his credit card. It appears your husband has been removed from all of your banking accounts with us."

"Ex-husband," I say, brushing my hair away from my face. "So that means everything is in my name now? Including all the debt?"

I knew today was too good to be true. Sal promotes me at work and now all of Austin's debt is going to be mine to deal with.

Sheila's eyebrows draw together as she types into her computer again. "Mrs…sorry, Ms. James, your credit card has a zero balance. It was paid in full the same day this paperwork was filed."

"What? No, that's not possible."

Spinning the computer monitor towards me she points to the screen. "See here, this is the credit card account, with a zero balance."

"I don't understand. What about the mortgage?"

"There is still a balance, but all the payments have been brought up to date. The late payment penalties have been cleared as well."

My eyes scan her screen frantically looking at the information. I must be dreaming. Any second, I'm going to wake up to a pile of bills.

Sheila places a hand gently on mine. "Listen, sugar, banks don't care where the money comes from when things are paid. There don't appear to be any errors here. So, I want you to go wipe those tears, straighten your shoulders, and walk out of here with your chin up. Good things happen to good people."

Nodding, I thank Sheila for her time. I graciously accept a printed copy of the credit card and mortgage statements. I'm still in shock as I sit in the parking lot looking over all the paperwork.

Did Austin do something responsible?

twenty-four
NOAH

"You're going to take a financial hit with this."

My financial advisor and his team of assistants watch me from across the conference room table. Felicia sits in the corner, next to my attorney.

"A small one, but it will be recouped within a year."

This meeting has already gone on longer than I like. I'm good at business, but I hate boardrooms. I hate wearing suits. I'm itching to get out of this thing. I need jeans, a t-shirt, and grease under my fingernails.

"That's a bold assumption." He straightens his glasses, reading over the business plan in front of him. "Relocating your corporate offices, there will be moving costs, and hiring new staff."

"Priorities have changed." My tone is firm, staring across the table. "The entire operation doesn't need to move. We can split work between two locations. But my personal office will be moving immediately."

"There is also the matter of selling your apartment," one of the younger assistants adds.

I'm pretty sure her name is Alexis. Smart, eager, and not afraid to speak up. I like her.

"All things I pay you to handle for me." I nod in her direction. "Felicia will oversee the arrangements for the offices as my new VP of operations."

I left this part of the meeting off the agenda that Felicia put together. A promotion I had been considering for awhile, but now it fits into my plan perfectly.

Felicia looks around the room with a confident stare, but I know she's surprised, which I'm enjoying.

"This meeting is simply a courtesy to let you know of my plan. Each of you still has a job, and I will continue to require your services. But I'll be leaving this as soon as possible."

I don't wait for replies or questions. The benefit of being the boss is I can end a meeting when I want. Boy, do I want this to end.

Buttoning my suit coat, I nod to everyone and then walk to my office. Felicia follows me, shutting the door behind her.

"VP of Operations?"

"You want to move and be my assistant?"

"Are there hot women where you're going?"

"Only one who matters." My lips curve at the thought of Sydney's blonde hair and full lips.

It's been almost two weeks since she left my room and snuck out before dawn. Missing her and Tyler is a never-ending tightness in my chest.

"I trust you, and you run this place without me anyway," I tell her while packing my personal items. "Are you going to redecorate?"

"Yeah, this office is too soft," she quips, "it lacks edge."

I laugh, shaking my head. "You're ok with handling

things? I'll be tied up with finding a new office and assistant."

"Nothing I can't handle." Felicia steps closer, resting her hands on the desk. "Does she know?"

"No."

"Gutsy move," she laughs, raising her eyebrows. "Works in my favor though. You leaving town leaves more ladies for me."

"I'll miss you too."

"Hmm," she huffs before opening the office door but stops for a second. "Don't fuck it up, no take backs on the office."

Promoting her was the right choice because I wasn't kidding when I said I would be busy. My plans aren't just business related. There will be a lot of humble groveling to make Sydney mine. And Tyler, too. Although, I feel like he will take far less effort.

The rest of the afternoon flies by as I busy myself with packing. My apartment will be handled by movers, and my suitcase was already taken to the airport. After several in-office visits and phone calls about employee retention, I finalize my day before drafting a company email.

Subject: Company changes
 From: Noah Reed, CEO

By now many of you have discovered our corporate structure is changing. Effective immediately, Felicia Jackson will be our new Vice President of Operations. She has been a trusted employee for many years, and I have full faith in her abilities.

Also, effective immediately my personal office will be moving. Being closer to my family has become a higher priority. I want to assure you that your jobs are safe. Currently there is no discussion of closing this office. I will be looking for staff at my new location. Anyone interested in relocating can reach out to human resources for more information. You will be hired at your current position and salary with moving compensation.

Respectfully,
N. Reed

twenty-five
SYDNEY

Thank goodness it's Friday. My first full week as manager has been busier than I would have imagined. Even after years of working here, I'm learning new things like the payroll software for one.

I'm punching the keyboard and cursing the person who invented this system. It's a wonder I ever received a paycheck if this is what Sal had to deal with.

My cell phone rings before I can yell the string of profanities at the computer monitor.

"Hello?"

"Sydney James?"

"Yes."

"This is Erika from family court. I'm calling to let you know the change in custodial status has been approved by the judge. Your certified copies are ready for pickup."

"I'm sorry, what?" I must have heard her wrong. I submitted all the paperwork after the divorce was finalized over a year ago.

A call from family court turns my stomach.

"Your custodial change forms. Our office closes at five

on the dot. Please bring photo identification." Erika hangs up before I can ask any more questions.

What if Austin signed over the house so he could file for custody of Tyler?

My heart races as I grab my purse and keys. "Lou! I need to go; something has come up. I'll be back if I can."

I'm out the door and running to my car before he even replies. I frantically scroll through my phone to find the number for the attorney I used during the divorce.

"Prescott Family Law," a man's voice greets on the other end of line.

I'm almost annoyed at how calm he sounds as if he should already know what the call is about.

Doing my best to relax, I focus on the road in front of me. "Yes, can I speak with Mr. Prescott please?"

"I'm sorry, but he's in court today. May I be of some assistance or take a message for him?"

"My name is Sydney James. He represented me for my divorce last year. The family court just called about changes in the custodial paperwork for my son. I didn't make any changes. I'm worried my ex is trying to do something."

With every word, my pulse speeds up as does the car. Thankfully, I'm still aware of some surroundings like the approaching stop sign. My hands shake as I spill everything over the phone.

I hear the tapping of a keyboard on the other end of the phone. "I do see some changes were made within your case file. Unfortunately, I'm not able to discuss them with you. I will have Mr. Prescott call you as soon as possible. Have a nice day, ma'am."

"That's it?" I scream into my phone, but the call is already disconnected.

Ten painfully long minutes later, I'm standing at the

counter in the family court records department. Luck smiles on me when the name tag of the woman sitting behind the counter reads "Erika".

"Can I help you?" she tonelessly greets. Family court seems like a thankless job.

"I think you may have called me a little while ago. My name is Sydney James."

"Identification please," she says, not taking her eyes off her computer.

With my driver's license in hand, she turns toward another counter and grabs a manila envelope. "These are certified copies of the paperwork. Any errors will need to be submitted for correction with a twenty-dollar charge for re-certification. You have thirty days from today to make said corrections."

The envelope and my ID are shoved into my hands as her eyes already fixes on the person behind me in line.

"Well, wait, what changes were made? Do I owe anything for these? Because I'm not paying for something I didn't request."

"Ma'am," she says, glaring at me. "I work in records. I'm not allowed to read or discuss court matters with you. The computer says there is no fee. Next customer, please."

Just like that I'm dismissed.

Finding a bench in the hallway, I close my eyes and try to steady my nerves. Whatever it says inside will have to be handled calmly. The acid in my stomach continues to rise as I rip the seal and take out the paperwork.

Petition to terminate parental rights.

My eyes scan the document that lists Austin James as the petitioner with his signature scrolled across the bottom. He gave up his son.

For a moment my heart shatters for Tyler. A father is

supposed to be his son's best friend, but Austin just signed him away.

Then a new thought hits me. I have sole custody of my son. Austin will never be able to fight me for him. Of course, that also means he'll never give me child support, not that he ever has.

A name at the bottom of the paper catches my eye. "Prepared by Steinwick & Morgan law offices." The name sounds too expensive for anyone Austin could hire. If I remember correctly his divorce attorney has a billboard that advertises divorce and personal injury services.

I use my phone to google the law office and call the number listed. After several rings, an older woman with the slightest British accent answers.

"Good afternoon, Steinwick & Morgan law offices, how may I direct your call?"

"I'm sorry I'm not sure who I need to speak with. It appears some custody papers were prepared by your law office, and I don't know why."

"I see, may I have your name please?"

"Sydney James."

"Um, I'm sorry I'm not finding anything. Why don't you leave me your number, and I'll inquire around the office to find out more?"

After giving her my number, I tuck everything in my purse and make my way out of the courthouse. The air somehow feels warmer and fresher. The weight of being tied to Austin is no longer on my shoulders. It's a sense of freedom I didn't know I was looking for.

Sitting in my car, I decide on one more google search and type Noah's name into my phone. His picture fills the screen, and my stomach does a cartwheel. His dark eyes looking back at me sends a shiver down my spine.

Scrolling past the photos, I find a link to his company

website. There are tabs to every department in the company, including the legal department. One click redirects me to a different website.

"Son of bitch," I whisper to no one.

The name Steinwick & Morgan appears in a bold powerful font across the screen. Scrolling back to his company site, I find the number for his office and hit dial without thinking twice.

"Jensen Automotive, how may I help you?"

I'm tired of chipper people answering phone calls. It's not their fault though; they are paid to be the friendly voice. But the emotional rollercoaster ride I'm on is sick of their positivity.

"I need to speak with Noah Reed right now."

The woman on the other end sounds a bit nervous. "I'm sorry but Mr. Reed is not in the office. May I connect you to his voicemail?"

"No," I state flatly, no use for pleasantries at this point. "When will he be in?"

"Mr. Reed has moved his office. He'll be unreachable until a new location is established. I can connect you to our vice president of operations."

"No thank you." I say, hanging up the call.

Noah moved? Trying his cell phone proves useless as my call goes straight to voicemail. Maybe I could talk to his parents about how to reach him. I'm willing to bet Sharon would call him and do the yelling for me if I told her everything.

I head to his parents' place after picking up Tyler from school. Tyler can't control his excitement as we pull into the Reeds' driveway. Mike is tinkering in the garage

He smiles wide, waving happily when he notices us.

"This is a nice surprise," he says, bending down to scoop Tyler in for a hug. "What are you doing here?"

"Mama says she needs to have grown up talk with you. But I want to play."

Mike's smile fades as he looks at me. "Everything ok?"

"I need to get a hold of Noah."

Mike's eyes narrow as if he's confused as he looks between me and Tyler.

"He's in his room upstairs."

twenty-six
NOAH

The door to my bedroom opens with such force I'm positive the hinges have come off. Spinning around from my desk I'm struck. Not in a metaphorical sense. I'm physically struck in the face with an envelope.

"You son of a bitch," Sydney yells, planting her hands firmly on her hips.

I know she's mad, but my cock twitches at the sight of her. Her blue eyes blaze with fire. The way her chest rises and falls is hypnotic. I would be playing with fire if I told her how hot she looks, but what a way to go.

"Hello to you, too," I quip, looking at the documents inside the envelope. "You should be careful; I may have gotten a paper cut."

"That will be the nicest thing that happens to you right now."

Her hostility isn't completely unwarranted, but Austin was dragging her down with him and his debt. Even though I went behind her back, paying him off and running him out of town was the best option. Now, I just need to make her see it that way.

SAFE WITH ME

I'm still in my suit and tie, only having arrived home a few moments before she rushed in. Standing from my desk, I loosen my tie.

"Do you mind if I get comfortable? I've been in this all day."

"Fine, but I have things to say to you."

"By all means, poppy," I say, tugging at the Windsor knot. "What do you want to tell me?"

"I know your attorney drew up the custody papers."

"Yes, they did." I slowly drag the tie from around my neck, looking her in the eye.

There's a flash of heat behind the anger. I watch her swallow hard. "Why would you ask Tyler's father to do that to him?"

"Austin didn't bat an eye, Sydney. He was a useless pile of shit who would never love and support his son."

Her eyes track my every move as I untuck my blue dress shirt from my pants. They roam over me like a piece of candy in a display window.

"What about the things with the bank?" Her eyes finally meet mine again.

"My doing as well." I start to unbutton my shirt slowly while taking calculated steps towards her. "I also paid off Austin's bookie." One more step, one more button. "And paid for him to leave town."

"I told you I didn't want you to make choices for me."

Another step, another button. "Maybe I'm not doing this all for you." With the front of my shirt open, I work on the sleeves. Undoing each cuff link, rolling the first sleeve up my arm. "Perhaps, I have a selfish motive." The material is tight against my forearm, as I move to the next one.

Sydney begins to take slow steps backward as I stalk toward her. "What do you get out of this?"

"You and Tyler." With both sleeves rolled, I take my

last step toward her, caging her against the wall. "With Austin gone, I can make you mine for good."

"You did things behind my back." Sydney raises her chin to glare at me. "Are you going to keep doing things without talking to me? What kind of relationship is that? What next, Noah?"

"I moved here for you," I tell her, my arms still firmly on the wall. "I sold my apartment, packed everything I own, and moved here."

"You moved? Here?" she asks, searching my eyes.

"I did." I lean in closer, my lips hovering over hers. "I'll pay off a thousand assholes and move anywhere to have you for myself."

"Noah, this is—"

"I love you, Sydney Parker." I toss in her maiden name to get her full attention. "I have loved you since the day you sat next to me in class. The hot cheerleader getting paired up with the outcast. It was my dream come true back then."

"And now," she asks, biting her lower lip. "What's your dream now?"

Smiling, I close the door next to her and turn the lock with a satisfying click. "You."

I crash my lips into hers, stealing whatever words she was going to say. I'm done talking and need to feel her against me. Her fingertips brush against my abs just above my waistband. The skin under her touch tingles.

Sydney moans against my lips as I tangle my fingers in her hair. Pulling her head back, I press myself against her body.

"Are we done fighting now?" I whisper into her ear.

"No," she whispers back before grabbing my belt. "But I'm willing to pause the conversation."

Groaning with frustration, I push away from the wall

and cup her cheeks in my hands. "I did what I did, because I couldn't stand to watch you work so hard while he fucked you over. You and Tyler deserve so much better."

"But I deserve to have a say in the conversation, Noah."

"As long as you and Tyler are safe, I can agree to that."

Sydney's smile tells me everything I need at this moment. Our lips find each other again. Hers part for me, allowing my tongue to dive into her mouth. Hands roam over skin as articles of clothing are tossed to the ground. In all of the spinning and laughing, we've made our way to the edge of the bed.

"On your knees, face the headboard," I command, turning her away from me.

She happily scrambles onto the bed with her perfectly plump ass wiggling back and forth. When she parts her knees to show me her perfectly glistening pussy, my control is almost lost.

My thumb circles her clit before drawing between her slit. So wet, so perfect. "Do you still want to try new things?"

"As long as you touch me." She's already panting under my soft touch. Her hips gently push back to gain more friction.

"I'm going to do more than just touch you, poppy." I lean over to kiss along the back of her neck. "You wanted a say in things. So, tell me if you want to keep trying new things."

"Yes."

Using my fingers and thumb, I continue to rub along her wet opening. Her moans and gasps increase with each stroke of my hand. Each time drawing my hand further up until I circle her tight rear. My hand is dripping with her arousal, which I swirl around the puckered opening.

Her body stiffens for a moment.

"It's ok, poppy. Remember anything you don't like we stop."

She nods her head in understanding as I continue massaging her. Gently probing with the tip of my thumb. "Relax, poppy. Just relax your hips and push back against my finger when you're ready."

Sydney takes a deep breath before her hips push backward. My thumb pushes past the outer rim of her ass. She pauses for a moment, exhaling as she sinks back.

Precum is already dripping from my cock as I gently move my thumb back at forth. Hearing her breathing change, her moans growing in strength. Fisting my cock with my other hand, I look at Sydney who watches over her shoulder.

Her eyes locked on my cock as she licks her lips.

"You want this?" I ask, squeezing as I run my hand up and down my length.

"Yes." She lets out a breathy response, her eyelids becoming heavy with need.

Sliding my head along her slit, I delight in the sinful heat of her dripping pussy. Aligning myself with her opening, I sink deep inside her. Stilling myself as she adjusts to being so full.

"Noah, this...this is...oh, please move your hips. I want to feel all of it." Sydney moves her hips back and forth, taking my cock, while I finger her ass.

"That's it, poppy. Take everything you want from me." My hips begin to match her thrusts. Slowly I replace my thumb with a finger, pushing deeper and stretching her tight opening.

She screams in ecstasy. Her body slick with sweat, tits bouncing with each thrust. When she throws her head back, her hair covering her back, a sinful scream coming from her mouth.

"Harder, Noah," she cries, gripping the comforter.

My free hand grabs her hip as I slam against her and find a rhythm with my cock and finger. Stretching her, claiming her in every way.

The corners of my vision begin to blur and stars appear before my eyes as Sydney begins to contract around me. Her climax comes without warning as she squeezes tight. My name flowing from her lips over and over.

I spill inside her in waves, never slowing my pace. Just as the last spurt is about to spill, I pull out and come all over her ass. Watching it drip down her crack gives me the greatest sense of possession.

She's *mine*.

Spreading my cum along her tight hole, I notch my still hard crown at her entrance. Sydney smiles when she looks over her shoulder, nodding her approval. With slow pressure, I push past her tight rim and slide deeper as she adjusts to me.

"Oh, yes," she moans, her hands moving to her clit. "Fuck me like that, Noah."

Surprising myself that I remain rock hard inside her ass, I let her move along my shaft. Syd doesn't hold back, moving back to meet my hips.

Our hands work together to fuck her pussy. Her fingers rubbing her clit while I slide two fingers inside. When we both come, it's explosive. She gushes all over the bed as I fill her ass.

When we collapse onto the mattress, neither of us can speak. Our breathing ragged as we stare at one another.

"You're mine, poppy," I finally whisper, pulling her body to mine.

She doesn't say anything before getting up and walking

to the bathroom. I watch with satisfaction as my cum runs down her legs.

After stripping the bed of the soaked linen, I join her in the shower and wait for her reply.

She smiles as her hands glide over me. When her ocean blue eyes finally find mine, she makes me whole.

"I love you too."

epilogue
SYDNEY

One year later

"Are you sure this is what you want to do?" Noah asks me for the tenth time this morning.

The first few times was after I pulled out a new battery-operated toy and asked him to use it on me. He's been a very willing participant in my sexual exploration. Of course, it benefits him as well, which is why he loves doing it.

"I'm sure, thank you for checking." I lean over the console of the car to kiss his cheek. "Have I told you today that I love you?"

"Does moaning it count?" he says with a sly wink.

"Mmm, I'm good with that." His lips find mine, and I'm ready to jump in his lap. "If we don't stop, this will never happen."

"Ok, to be continued." Noah gets out of the car, running around to open my door.

The last year has been like nothing I could ever imagine. When he returned home, Noah decided to build a house instead of buying an apartment because he wanted a place for us when I was ready to take that step.

He asked for my opinion on everything from the flooring to the light fixtures. I didn't want to believe he was building it for me, but that's exactly what he was doing.

When the house was completed six months ago, he asked me and Tyler to move in. On moving day, he proposed on the front step of our home. It was perfect in every way. He even had Tyler help pick out the ring. I love the way it sparkles when his hand is holding mine.

Noah opened a small office here with a few staff members, continuing to run his main operations from corporate headquarters. He still travels there once a month, but never for more than a few days, because being away from us makes him anxious.

I continue to manage the diner and expanded our outreach with the soup kitchen. We've received donations from many local businesses, including Jensen Automotive. Noah offered to fund the whole project, and while it's a generous idea, I love involving the community. It has become bigger than ever, and we're looking at leasing a commercial building to have a full-time soup kitchen.

Stepping onto the porch of my little house, I can't help but feel a bit sad. After all, this is where I brought my baby home from the hospital. A place where he had so many firsts. But the time has come to let it go along with the bad memories it holds.

"Here come the new owners," Noah whispers, wrapping his arms around my waist.

Thomas and his wife pull up with their precious baby girl, Ruby. When I decided to sell, I knew it would be a good starter home for a young family. It was by luck that Thomas was looking for a house and Mike and Noah made minor renovations to make it perfect.

The proud young parents beam with pride as they step onto the front walk. Ruby babbles in her mama's arms.

"Congratulations on your first home," I tell them, holding the keys up. "We put a welcome home basket inside, and if there are any issues, you know how to reach me."

After some hugs and a quick goodbye, Noah and I are off to the second important task of the day. The sun shines, and warm spring air breezes through the open windows and blows my hair around. Noah's fingers rubs the top of my leg.

"You're a little quiet," I say, looking over at him.

"Just thinking." His smile is sexy and warms me from head to toe.

"What are you thinking?"

"I want to put a baby in you."

A slow smile curls the corners of my mouth. "I think we can work on that."

Noah pulls over to the side of the road and puts the car in park.

"Noah, I didn't mean right now."

"I know, you dirty girl." He pulls my hand to his lips. "But, you're serious? You're ok with the idea of a baby?"

"Ideally, I would want to wait until after the wedding. But I'll call the doctor about having my IUD removed." I squeeze his hand. "I would love to have your baby."

"We should practice making one soon," he says, adjusting his pants. "Now put away the sexy look, we have important business to take care of."

I laugh as he pulls back onto the road.

Pulling up to our destination, a nervous flutter begins in my stomach. This is a very big step for all of us. Noah looks more nervous than when he proposed.

"Hey, it's going to be great," I tell him, running my finger through his hair.

"What if—"

"It's going to be ok, Noah. I promise."

Walking hand in hand, Noah and I climb the steps to the courthouse. Sharon and Mike are already inside with Tyler, who kicks his feet back and forth while he sits patiently on the bench.

Noah takes a deep breath before kneeling in front of Tyler.

"Hey, buddy," he says calmly. "Do you know what we're doing here?"

"Was I bad? Do I have to go to jail?" Tyler asks, holding his teddy bear close. "Ben Smith says when you go to the courthouse, you go to jail."

We all chuckle as his little eyes look for reassurance.

I kneel next to Noah in front of him. "No, sweetheart, nobody is going to jail."

Except for maybe Austin who was arrested in Nevada for illegal gambling and drug charges. I dodged a major bullet thanks to Noah's interference, which he likes to remind me about from time to time.

"Tyler." Noah glances at me first before continuing. "We're here because I want to adopt you."

"What does 'adopt' mean?"

"Well, buddy, it means I would be your dad."

"Forever?" Tyler sits up straighter, his eyes wide.

"Yeah, forever. No matter what, you'll be my son and I'll be your dad."

"What do you think, sweetheart?" I ask gently.

Tyler puts his little hand to his chin, suddenly looking

less like my little boy and more like a big kid. He looks around at the four adults surrounding him. Three who chose to be part of his life, because he's that special.

"Can we get ice cream after?"

"Are you negotiating with me?" Noah asks, cocking his head to the side.

"Well, I *am* going to be your kid."

Noah's chest swells with pride as he wraps his arms around Tyler. Everyone has tears in their eyes, except maybe Tyler who just wants ice cream.

I watch as the judge reads over the adoption papers and talks to Noah and Tyler about what it all means before finally looking at me.

"And you, as the boy's mother, agree to the legal adoption of the minor child by Noah Reed."

"Yes, your honor."

Through all the twists and turns life takes before leading you to where you should be, I never thought the road would lead here.

Noah is going to be the father of my son, my husband, and it all started with a random partner assignment in high school. One that could have been changed if I asked the teacher, but there was something about Noah. He may not have been popular or athletic, but he was comforting.

Noah has always known who he is, never compromising that for the sake of other people's opinions. He spent years hiding in school to avoid the bullies and later as an adult to avoid those with ulterior motives. The painful truth in that would be enough to destroy most, but Noah is stronger than anyone.

Now, he's going to teach Tyler how to be the same kind of man. A man who loves unconditionally, which is how I know we'll be safe with him.

"Come on, poppy. Let's take our son for ice cream."

. . .

— The End —

thank you for reading!

Like you, I have fallen head over heels for the romance genre. Reading and writing romance has, in many ways, been healing for me. I love what I do and hope to be able to write many more stories like this.

If you enjoyed Sydney and Noah's story, please consider leaving a review or telling a friend! Every little thing helps me on my self-publishing journey.

Until next time, happy reading!

about the author

Cindy Houghton is self-published author of contemporary romance stories. In 2023 she wrote and published two, with plans for many more. She mixes humor, sassy sarcasm, relatable topics, and plenty of steaminess to keep you interested.

Living in the Pacific Northwest with her family, she also enjoys photography and cooking. She spent five years working in Adult Corrections, giving her no shortage of interesting stories to share. Somehow between family life, a full-time job, and a love of reading romance novels, she works hard to bring characters to life on the page. Don't forget the coffee, which she lovingly refers to as "Go-Go Juice" and "The Nectar of the Gods", just don't offer her decaf.

CONNECT WITH CINDY HOUGHTON

facebook.com/cindyhoughton.books
instagram.com/cindyhoughton_author

acknowledgments

Short and sweet this time, I must acknowledge my two book besties.

Chessa, my editor and friend, who somehow turns my words into coherent thoughts. Your magic is endless, and I'm a better writer because of you. Thank you for opening chapters of opportunities for me and the positive feedback as I grow.

Ivy, my plant-loving sounding board. There is no amount of typed words to express my gratitude for you. From all the vent sessions, idea emails, and encouragement you provide, it's been amazing to get to know you.

I would be lost in this indie publishing world without the two of you.

also by cindy houghton

MEN OF MEHAMA

Sparking Romance (Book One)

Frozen Together (Book Two)

Book Three — Coming 2025

OTHER WORKS

Living Charlotte

Bad Liar Anthology

Head In The Clouds Anthology — August 2024

UPCOMING PROJECTS

Chameleon Rose — Late 2024

Printed in Great Britain
by Amazon